The silver knight

The Silver Knight

Lorenzo Rossi

This book is dedicated to all those who love Freedom and who fight every day to get It when they don't have It.

The silver knight

I

The knight dressed in red waited impatiently for the signal holding his spear towards the sun high in the sky.

His black horse, adorned with a saddle-cloth of the same colour as his rider, had a curious whitish spot in the shape of arrow on the muzzle and was very nervous and could not stand still in its position, so that, occasionally, it made rotational movements on itself by launching neighs that attracted the attention of everyone from the audience.

The warm air made the rider so restless that, at a certain point, he decided to raise the visor of his helmet to enjoy a few moments of coolness on his face.

He was thus able to better see his opponent who, unlike him, remained motionless on his white horse without showing signs of yielding to impatience.

The silvery colour of that knight's suit reflected the sunlight that was hitting his eyes directly, preventing him from fixing his gaze on his rival.

He knew who was in front of him and he was very proud to have reached the final with that opponent in that famous tournament.

That was a "game" that was traditionally played once at the height of summer, where competitors from anywhere were free to participate, knowing very well that it was a non-fatal challenge and that it was worth their honor and reputation.

Who of the two lost the spear or fell off the horse was the loser and the other the winner; if both fell off the horse, the game was repeated.

It was very simple and also quite safe because the challengers were harnessed with heavy armor and with a large shield, but above all for the fact that the spears were made of balsa wood, making them absolutely effective for this purpose, that is, to hit their opponent on the shield or armor causing it to fall to the ground without inflicting mortal damage.

A sound echoed in the air suddenly and the buzz of spectators was interrupted.

The two riders launched at full speed against each other, each with his own spear facing the contender.

The red rider hit the other on the shield making him jump backwards, taking an equally effective thrust on the right side of his metal armour, that was slightly dented.

The horses covered the entire route and, once they arrived at the starting point of their challenger, they stopped for a moment and, after the riders took a quick look, they returned to the charge with all their power.

Once they came face to face, the clash was as energetic as the previous one, but this time the two knights hit their spears which thus fell to the ground; then they were returned to them and the two contenders were able, in this way, to return to their starting point.

The silver knight raised the visor of his helmet to dry the sweat that fell from his forehead and the red knight did the same a few moments later.

The black horse suddenly reared up towards the sky and pawing with its front legs launched a heavy neigh which was the preamble for the start of a new duel.

Shortly afterwards the two riders lowered their visors and launched themselves once again against each other.

The silver knight's spear struck the shield of his challenger who, on the other hand, was unable to hit the other with his own weapon: the thrust bent the shield and made the red knight lose his balance, thus falling from the horse.

While the spectators shouted, some out of joy, others out of disappointment, the silver knight approached the man on the ground and, after getting off the horse, held out his hand to help him standing up; the red knight initially hesitated, then accepted the help and nodded in confidence, receiving the same gesture from the other.

II

The sound of the gurgling water was so pleasant that Anselm did not care too much about the fact that the sky was darkening and that day was drawing to a close: he loved so much to dip his legs in the cool waters of that brook during the hot summer days that his thoughts alienated him from reality.

The Solitary Torrent, this was the nickname that the inhabitants of Thedra gave to that snake of water that crawled along the plain, was a stream that originated from Silver Mount, an imposing mass of metamorphic rock of whitish colour on whose southern side there was an area devoid of vegetation which, in the sun, reflected its rays appearing a silvery shade, so shiny that it seemed to want to shelter from the admiring glances of the locals.

Anselm used the water of the brook for various purposes, including that of irrigating his vegetable field, and he devoted himself to this activity with great passion, often being helped by his wife Evelune, a very sweet and smart woman who knew make herself loved by all the inhabitants of the town.

Anselm was a very robust man who had developed that build thanks to the manual work he carried out every day, but his greatest skill was that of fighting, for which he enjoyed great fame in his town and in the neighboring territories.

His wife was a beautiful woman whom everyone envied because she had a face that was very difficult to forget for those lucky enough to be able to meet her in person and a body that seemed perfectly shaped, as if shaped by a divine hand.

"Come inside, Anselm...it's dark now!"

Hearing no response, Evelune looked out of the small wooden window and, peering eastward, saw a motionless silhouette immersed in the water that seemed to be more a wild animal than a man.

"So...did you go deaf?" exclaimed the woman

The motionless figure stood up and replied:

"Here I am, I will arrive immediately"

Both embraced under the growing gaze of the moon which, by now, illuminated the dark expanse of the valley.

Entering their welcoming home, Anselm sat on his usual dark wooden chair, facing the large round table in the center of the entrance hall, which had been created by his father, obtained from an enormous centuries-old oak tree that was located near the nearby Intricate Wood, an immense and very intricate forest that few men went through leaving it unscathed. On the back there was an indefinite symbol, carved to a depth of about three millimeters, which seemed to be a tree or a plant with very sparse branches, but Anselm had never understood what it was exactly and what it meant, provided that it had a meaning.

The interior of the house was very welcoming and everything was made from wood and stone from the quarries of Silver Mount; the small windows allowed the light to illuminate the interior rooms sufficiently without it being too intrusive and were mostly facing south-east.

"Look what a beautiful moon there is tonight," Evelune said looking at the sky from a window

"I felt so good outside" he replied, giving her a smile

"If you want, let's go and observe the stars" continued the woman, touching her long blond braids that she always kept well-groomed and almost perfect.

"Come here..." Anselm said taking her hand... "you know you are very beautiful..."

"Sometimes you have to tell me" she replied, looking at him straight in his eyes

"But if I tell you every day..." he replied

"I like it when you tell me..." she said giving him a kiss

Anselm stood up from the chair and accompanied Evelune out, after which they both lay down on the grass, right in front of the door, looking at the immensity of the sky.

"Look at that star over there!" Evelune shouted full of enthusiasm

"It seems easy..." he said laughing

"What do you mean?" she retorted, turning her face towards him

Anselm looked at her and observed, enchanted, her eyes illuminated by the penetrating moonlight and showing the splendid turquoise color that further embellished those wonderful eyes that characterized her.

"Well...what are you looking at?"

"The most beautiful star is you!"

"Stop that! I meant that up there!" Evelune said, pointing to a star to the northwest that seemed to shine more than the others.

"But the sky is full of them...how can I understand which one you mean?".

They began to discuss which star was the brightest one and, while the two spoke on the grass immersed in the night, suddenly the surrounding silence was broken by a sudden noise coming from some shrubs located about twenty meters from them.

The two stood up and peered towards that point but could not see anything.

"It could be a boar..." Anselm said

Evelune took a few steps back trying to drag him too but Anselm motioned to her to be silent; he ran quickly into the house, went to the fireplace at the bottom of the large hall and grabbed Aglet, the great sword of the legendary Brom, a knight of the north who, according to ancient legends, would have killed the great bear of the eastern lands, the much feared Kardeth, a ferocious beast that terrified the peoples of those areas in times long gone.

Running out, he invited Evelune to step back and find protection inside the house, not giving her any chance to reply.

Advancing in the dark, he tried to pick up some noise from behind the vegetation but the only thing he heard was the barely audible rustle of the wings of a huge owl that fluttered a few meters from his head.

A few steps from the shrubs, Anselm grasped the hilt of the broadsword with his two hands, preparing to launch an attack with the mighty weapon.

Evelune watched the scene from the door with great anguish.

Anselm, with a lightning bolt, swooped behind the vegetation and, warily, made sure that nothing was there.

"It is very strange...something made noise a little while ago..." he said to himself.

He waited a few moments in the silence and, while he was crouching, the thought turned to Evelune and so, leaning very cautiously, he glanced towards the house but, apart from the half-open door, he could not notice anything else; everything seemed quiet around him and nothing could be heard from the nearest houses, everyone seemed to sleep in peace.

Absorbed in his thoughts, he did not notice that behind him, just above his head, two huge round yellow eyes watched him with great intensity and the head of that being moved to the right and left at an irregular rhythm.

It was a mighty eagle owl intent on perhaps searching for some prey and which was perched on a branch of the big elm that overlooked those shrubs.

"If you were the one I saw a few seconds ago, it means that..." the man said to himself

"Ahh...what I am saying...it must have been another owl..." his mind continued

Realizing that time had passed, Anselm got up and, with the same great caution, directed his stealthy steps towards his house.

Arriving in front of the main entrance, he took a last look over there towards those plants and, surrendering to the evident mystery, entered inside exclaiming:

"I only saw an owl staring at me..."

Nobody answered him.

"Evelune!"

The living room was empty but the door has remained open.

"Hey...where are you?" he repeated shouting and heading for the kitchen.

There was nobody there too.

Then, placing the sword on the large round table in the room, he ran to the other rooms but also in this case the result was always the same.

His heart began to beat faster, he no longer knew what was happening.

It occurred to him that perhaps she might have gone out to look for him, and that's why the door had remained open.

As he was about to go out, he noticed a sheet of paper that had been attached to the door with a dagger: his blood froze.

"We won't hurt her, but you have to come to the Intricate Wood tomorrow night...alone."

The sheet had no other writing, had no signature...Anselm fell on his knees, disconsolate because he didn't know what to do.

"Why did I leave her alone?" he said aloud.

Struck by great anguish, he ran outside and, regardless of everything around him, went to the small stable next to the house to saddle Aster, his beautiful white horse that he needed for moving, in particular to go to the mount Silver and carry useful material for the home.

While he was addicted to doing this, he heard a noise a few steps behind him and then spun around.

"What are you doing here?" he said in a surprised voice.

"I heard screams and so..." replied the other

"I'm sorry, Cyr...but I have to go" Anselm said

"In the middle of the night? Where do you have to go?" Cyr continued

"I'm in a hurry..." he replied trying to cut the speech

"Why did you call Evelune? Where is she?"

"Uhm...well..." Anselm stammered

"what happened? Tell me! " the other insisted

"They kidnapped her!" Anselm whispered annoyed

"Kidnapped? And who?"

"I don't know...I don't know how it could have happened, in such a short time...we were out here enjoying the starry night when we heard a noise coming from those shrubs over there! It was a strange noise, as if there was a big animal...or someone...I don't know..."

"And then what happened?" Cyr asked

"I went to see what there was behind it, but I didn't see anyone..."

"Maybe they wanted to distract you!"

"It is probable but now there is no time to waste!"

"I'll come with you!" Cyr said

"absolutely not!" Anselm replied

"You may need..."

"no!" he said resolutely

Cyr remained silent without insisting further.

He was a great friend of Anselm and sometimes went to Mount Silver with him because the mountain environment regenerated him: he loved to feel his feet touch the bare rock and breathe that air so pure, pungent that intoxicated him, he delighted in climbing up the narrow paths that led to the top and up there he was not afraid of anything, even when he was with precipices hundreds of meters deep behind him, in fact he often voluntarily went to look for all those strange and little places known by others for a simple spirit of adventure that characterized him.

Cyr was not a man like any other, he belonged to the race of the dwarves, he was slightly taller than a meter and came from the distant lands of the south, where the people of the dwarves are said to still reside, and he had moved to Thedra because "longing to discover new lands", as he himself tells all those who ask him, but then, in love with those wonderful places, he chose to stay there.

What mainly characterized him was the long beard he wore and which was divided into two parts, each tied to the waist-band, and this had been for a long time the object of ridicule by many inhabitants of Thedra but then, over time, he knew how to win their respect in an excellent way.

Anselm had just finished preparing the horse that ran into the house, grabbed his crossbow, took a bottle which he filled with fresh spring water, some homemade biscuits and, slamming the door, jumped on Aster's back.

"Uhm...where are you going?" Cyr asked with great curiosity

"They are waiting for me at the Intricate Forest!" he answered giving a grooming to the horse

"But that forest is..."

Cyr couldn't finish the sentence that the knight was already galloping.

The dwarf watched Anselm leave quickly in the night and suddenly an idea occurred to him.

He ran to his house, grabbed his large ax which he used to cut down trees and get firewood and, before you could say Jack Robinson, mounted his horse and headed for the forest at great speed.

Anselm spurred Aster by urging it to run and felt all the power of the animal: the regular noise of the hooves hitting the ground seemed so vigorous to him that it was as if a handful of warriors on horseback were around him.

The wind lifted the animal's long white mane that sometimes it covered the rider's sight, but Anselm was so uneasy that he didn't even notice that.

On the way the rider observed the large grassy expanse that surrounded him: it was an immense field of crucifers plants which, whenever the wind blew over it, appeared as an endless sea of dark green color whose waves favoured the gait of the horse towards an unknown shore.

That shore was represented by the forest and Anselm saw it closer and closer.

Reaching about a hundred meters from it, the rider drew the bridles and Aster finally slowed its frenzied race by launching an energetic neigh in the air that echoed until it penetrated that wall of gigantic trees.

Anselm lingered a few moments to inspect the edge of the forest and took advantage to drink a sip of fresh water; having identified a point where the trees seemed to want to welcome the wandering travelers, the knight grabbed the crossbow armed with an arrow and entered the dreaded forest.

Giant oaks and majestic birches made up the majority of the trees of the Intricate Wood and they intertwined so clearly that they seemed to be an army of trunks with a single endless crown.

Inside, as there were so many trees that it seemed to be in a closed place, there was an intense intoxicating smell of fresh foliage that made the air almost pungent, moreover there was an extraordinary sensation of coolness that Anselm felt immediately and appreciated very much, considering the diurnal heat that characterized those days in the height of summer.

The call of some unknown nocturnal bird broke the silence into many more or less long pieces and that kind of songs from the most secret hiding places scattered here and there in the middle of the woods, made the atmosphere unusual, since the disturbing notoriety that it held was in stark contrast to the sweet melody of those calls.

Going far enough to no longer see the grassy plain behind him, Anselm began to wonder if he should have found them or if they would have found him: he expected the second thing and also expected that, for having kidnapped Evelune, those men had somehow need him. And this implied that if they had seen him, they certainly would not have killed him...but this was his thought and he certainly was not sure that this was true.

In addition, the danger could come from any ferocious animals, deadly traps or other men who did not belong to the group of the kidnappers of Evelune.

So Anselm advanced cautiously and with the crossbow ready to fire the dart.

III

When it was already three in the morning and the air had cooled further, Anselm began to feel the weight of sleep and tiredness therefore he decided to stop for a moment; he got off his horse at that point where some oaks with a twisted trunk seemed to form a circle around a small clearing.

He grabbed his bottle and took a small sip and then rinsed his face to refresh himself.

While he was intent on adjusting the saddle, he heard a barely audible noise coming from the top of the oak tree just above him; he immediately took the crossbow and pointed it upwards, waiting in silence.

What appeared to his eyes made him smile and led him to withdraw the weapon; a curious reddish squirrel was observing the man with eyes full of curiosity: Anselm took a biscuit from the bag that contained them and placed it on a branch. Moving away from it, he went to the opposite side of the clearing to take a look at the surrounding environment and understand if there was a path that led to somewhere.

He took a few steps on the ground covered with foliage and broken sticks when, suddenly, the ground collapsed into a pit approximately four meters deep: Anselm found himself submerged by damp soil in that huge hole.

"My poor head..." the man complained

"And now...how do I get out of here? I will never be able to..." he said to himself trying to jump and cling to something.

The huge hole had wooden planks that served as walls, demonstrating the fact that it was a man-made trap; the attempt to climb a wall was vain and Anselm was taken by total discomfort.

"Where's my sword?" the knight wondered

Digging into that pile of earth he first found his crossbow and, a little further on, under some broken oak branches, he saw the blade of a sword.

Anselm's morale was in low spirits, indeed, it was appropriate to say it: it was even underground.

"Uhm...what am I doing here...I should have been at home with Evelune..." he said to himself.

The knight threw his sword to the ground and began to scream, venting all his anger, so every other noise was covered by his desperate screams and the birds, for a few minutes, interrupted those wonderful singing competitions.

The squirrel to which he had fed was frightened by that scream and, with a lightning bolt, made some leaps reaching the top of the big oak tree in a few moments, disappearing into the darkness.

A few moments later, in the ghostly silence of that dark wood, a voice whispered from the edge of the cavity:

"Anselm!"

The knight was caught by surprise and with an incredulous look he peered upwards and saw the silhouette of a human figure protruding from the edge.

"Grab this branch, Anselm!" the unknown man said in a reassuring voice

"who are you? I can't see anything..." the knight replied, taking the earth off him

"I'm Cyr...don't you recognize me?"

"What are you doing here? I told you not to follow me..."

"If I hadn't, at this hour you would be trapped in here..." the dwarf replied

"Someone dug this trap and covered it perfectly...I couldn't avoid it..." the knight continued

"Hurry up! cling to the branch!"

Anselm threw his sword and crossbow at Cyr, then grabbed that sturdy oak branch and finally began to rise to the surface.

"If you hadn't launched that cry I don't know if I would have found you...this is a damned maze" Cyr said

"Yeah...I had never penetrated into it so much" the knight replied

"I hate forests, I prefer mountains...in the middle of the rocks I feel much safer"

"Cyr...I don't know what to do anymore...how do I find Evelune?"

"I don't know...let's go on, there could be the home of those cowards"

"But...there is no direction here, you have to go at random"

Cyr looked around in the dark and had a shiver of terror that froze his blood.

The increasing humidity inside the forest meant that a light layer of fog enveloped the surrounding environment so as to make visibility even more reduced.

"Let's continue on this way...I don't like this forest...it has eyes everywhere" Cyr exclaimed in a worried voice

The two mounted on horseback and decided to proceed keeping a distance of a few meters between themselves in order to prevent both from falling into the same possible trap.

Aster was very restless and sometimes it launched some neigh which cut through the fog and echoed in the vastness of the forest.

At a certain point the vegetation began to change and large beech trees with a whitish trunk emerged from the fog and were so thick that the two established that it was more appropriate to continue on foot rather than drive the horses crazy.

The ground became more and more irregular and more or less rounded brown rocks began to emerge and covered with thick tufts of dark green moss that made them slippery but at the same time very intoxicating for their delicious smell.

Suddenly Cyr stopped his pace by fixing a specific point on the ground, right in front of him.

"What's wrong with you now, Cyr?"

"I'm not sure but..."

The dwarf bent to the ground and reached out very cautiously, feeling what appeared to be a rope abandoned there on the ground; sniffing the deception, Cyr took a few steps away and looked for a fairly long branch nearby.

Near a young birch he noticed a broken branch that was right for him and then took it with him and returned to the point where he was before.

Keeping a certain distance, Cyr stretched out his arm and with his stick he pulled that rope which, in a heartbeat, snapped and a net, previously invisible, went up at high speed upwards carrying a pile of leaves and all sorts of undergrowth.

It was tied to the trunks of some beech trees in such a way that it was not visible to anyone passing by and was also very resistant: it had to be able to withstand a weight of several kilos and, moreover, it reached a height such that anyone was to be up there and intended to cut those ropes, he would have made a fall of at least eight or nine meters.

Anselm stood with his mouth open, staring upward.

"Apparently it's full of traps here..." Cyr interrupted the silence

"But...I can't make sense of all this..." Anselm said

"I don't know but I think it has something to do with those scoundrels..."

"Let's not waste any more time" the knight replied

In the middle of a path that the two accidentally found, Anselm saw something on the ground that immediately caught his attention.

"This is the Evelune's shawl! They passed through here!" he exclaimed in a mixed tone between joy and pain.

"I hope they didn't hurt her" Cyr replied, looking at his friend's shiny eyes

The knight picked it up and, with infinite longing in his heart, set off continuing on the path.

All of a sudden, in front of them, four human figures, armed with swords and bows, emerged from the fog and ordered them to stop and get off the horses.

Anselm and Cyr did not even have time to grab their weapons from the speed with which the four strangers appeared out of nowhere, also because they were both immersed in their thoughts, especially after the discovery of the Evelune's shawl.

The two men dismounted and were immediately surrounded by the four who ordered them to continue.

They were all dressed in the same way: a long dark green tunic that hid the legs up to the calves, a silver chainmail under the robe and a green hat that ended with a thick coloured feather.

Taking possession of their horses and their weapons, the four followed Cyr and Anselm in silence.

The fog was thinning more and more and the forest now seemed to be populated only by beautiful birch trees with a whitish trunk that rose towards the sky for more than twenty meters.

Anselm was very worried because he did not know who these people were and if they had anything to do with his woman; for this reason, worn out by doubts, he turned and said, addressing one in particular:

"Where's Evelune?"

The one to whom his eyes were directed nodded with the sword so as to invite him to continue the way without asking too many questions, but Anselm did not give in and repeated insistently:

"Where did you take Evelune?"

One of the four men, being faced with his obstinacy, replied in an intimidating voice:

"If you go on without making a fuss you will see her again soon"

"What have you done to her?"

The same of the four men ordered him to be silent and that was how Anselm and Cyr continued their way by entering the deepest bowels of that immense forest that seemed to have no end.

After about an hour's walk, the small group abandoned that narrow path to turn in a direction that seemed to lead to an area even more rich in vegetation, where the numerous and magnificent wild rhododendrons could not escape the sight, full of lively flowers from more varied colours that gave off a smell so pleasant that it made you want to stop and catch them.

The night was drawing to a close and, albeit listlessly, the dim sunlight tried to make its way through the immense foliage of the trees.

And it was precisely with the dawn breaking that the small group finally arrived in what looked like a wide avenue flanked by very old birches and which ended after twenty meters through a natural arch created by two robust branches of those wonderful green giants.

IV

The amazement at what appeared unexpectedly in front of them, once they passed that arch, was clearly legible in the eyes of Anselm and Cyr: an immense white stone building stood right in front of them, completely immersed in the Intricate Forest.

The surrounding walls, about ten meters high, were decorated with battlements and were well defended by the presence of numerous guards armed with long bows; in the corners there were four imposing circular towers, on the tops of which the presence of many armed sentinels was clearly visible.

Anselm did not know of the existence of that fortress but, like him, no one else from Thedra knew it in fact the populations of those areas stayed away from the Intricate Wood because they thought it was inhabited by malevolent presences and, sometimes, only a few unfortunate people entered it without ever leaving it again.

The large portcullis gate was raised as they passed and, after crossing a path in the center of the inner courtyard of the walls, the two men were led in front of the majestic wooden door where, once opened, other armed guards always dressed at the same way awaited them so that they took them inside the building, until they reached the higher floors.

After reaching the end of a long and well-lit corridor, the guards knocked on a door and someone from inside ordered them to enter.

It was a large hall where, in the center, there was a rectangular table, around which three people were sitting and arguing while drinking something inside some glasses; the two men were invited to sit down while the guards headed towards the front door and, remaining on guard inside the room, closed the door very discreetly.

Upon entering, they had not noticed the presence of two other guards at the far end of the hall, in a less illuminated area, right near another door near an old wooden bookcase.

The long white walls were adorned with numerous paintings but one of these stood out decidedly over the others: it was the portrait of a man with a thick beard covering his neck and wearing a very bright golden-yellow dress with dark blue herringbone stripes.

It looked just like the figure at the head of the table who was drinking a sip of red wine while looking closely at the two guests.

"I told you to come alone..." that one said in a very resolute voice

"I had left..."

"I followed him later!" Cyr said interrupting his friend

"Well...it doesn't matter now" replied the man at the head of the table

"Where's Evelune?" Anselm asked anxiously

"She is changing, she will be here soon" he replied. "I am Kellar, lord of this palace" he continued sipping the last drops of wine.

"I guess you're Anselm..." he went on to address the young knight

"How do you know my name?" he asked

"I have heard rumors of your prowess with the use of the sword and, if this skill accompanies shrewdness and intelligence, then it means that I have the right person in front of me"

"right...to do what?" Anselm asked

"Eustace, my personal adviser, will explain it to you" Kellar replied

The man with the moustache to his right introduced himself and, after clearing his throat a little, began to speak:

"You will have to enter the castle of King Reginald and perform a task very..."

"Where is this...?" Anselm interrupted

"Let me finish explaining you...uhm...well, then...we will give you the clothes that his guards wear, we have some in our warehouse: you will have to enter the rooms of his residence in Elysande, a town south of the Intricate Wood, about a hundred kilometers from here, and find out the name of the spy he sent to our palace to know our moves; once you find out, you'll have to come back here..."

"All this for a name?" the knight said

"Reginald is a treacherous person who has been fighting against us for a long time because he would like to appropriate our palace to have full control of the forest, so that his men can safely cross it and use it as a communication route to the north. Recently, some of our riders have been attacked and killed in the forest, many others have disappeared without anyone knowing anything about them anymore..."

"But...why me? And why did you kidnap Evelune? " Anselm intervened again

"We know of your acts of heroism in defense of the inhabitants of Thedra, especially when you fought against the barbarians of the northern mountains who had descended from those hills to head south and conquer your lands...and you killed Hildebrand, their leader, a skilled warrior who feared no enemy with his ax..." suddenly intervened the third man, to the left of Kellar

"Ours is a certificate of esteem for you...now continue, Eustace" Kellar said interrupting Bryce, this was the name of his military adviser

"Well...you asked us why we captured your woman: if we had come to you to ask you to perform this task for us, for a fee, even a substantial one, would you have done it?" the moustached man asked

"I would never leave Evelune alone, it's too dangerous, and then...if I refused to go to Elysande?" the young knight answered

"I don't think you want to refuse, it would be a further demonstration of your great ability" the councilor refuted

"I want to see Evelune...I don't care about your proposal!" Anselm exclaimed fervently

Kellar turned his gaze to Eustace and nodded to him, after which the latter got up and went to the half-hidden door at the bottom of the hall leaving the room.

"Only you are able to complete that mission; no one else, if he were in danger, would be able to get out of there..." Kellar said to the knight

"We will keep Evelune here and take care of her until your return, Eustace will take care of her personally"

"Free her" the knight exclaimed, rushing towards him

Then Bryce intervened and tried to calm him and reassure him again.

"We were at peace at our house last night, and you came..." Anselm continued

"When it's all over we'll have a way to remedy" Kellar replied coldly

"Nothing will ever end because it won't even start..."

"You should..."

The door at the end of the hall opened and, behind Eustace, Evelune appeared in all her beauty, dressed in a long blue dress that touched the floor.

"Evelune" the knight exclaimed full of joy

"Anselm" the woman said exploding in a mixed cry between happiness and despair

"Did they hurt you?" he asked, fixing her beautiful turquoise eyes

"No...uhm...no..." she stammered

"tell me the truth"

"I passed out last night, forgive me...I couldn't..."

"It doesn't matter" he replied, hugging her

"How did you know I was here?" she asked

"They left a sheet of paper that said I had to go to the forest"

"Okay, that's enough...Eustace bring her back to her room!" Kellar ordered

"Nooo! Make her stay a little longer" the knight replied

Eustace, with the help of the guards, detached Anselm from the woman and brought her back to her room, locking it.

Meanwhile Anselm, who tried to follow her, received a blow to the head by a guard so that he passed out and fell to the ground.

Cyr was led, through a long corridor adorned with vases of various shapes and sizes and with ancient weapons hanging on the stone walls, into a fairly large room, furnished with a bed that seemed to have been in disuse for some time, a dark wooden wardrobe, a small table of the same material, above which there was the only small window that illuminated that room: Cyr did not arrive well to see what there was beyond that window and at first he was content to glimpse that immense sky of intense blue colour but then, driven by extreme curiosity, he climbed onto the table, opened the window and, looking out of the opening, he observed the view; the opening overlooked the southern side of the building, from which you could see the internal courtyard with warehouses for food supplies, the barn, the horse stables, a circular well at the bottom on the right, all surrounded by walls, beyond which you could see the green lush forest that concealed that immense fortress.

The dwarf heard that the guards, after locking the door, left the room quickly.

The thought of Cyr immediately went to Anselm, wondering what had happened after that clash and if he had ever agreed to carry out that mission.

When he opened his eyes, the young knight immediately felt a great ache behind his head and remembered what had happened to him; glancing around he realized that he was in a very large room that had two doors along the same wall while, in the opposite one, there were two large windows, one of which was half-open from which a very good smell came...it almost smelt like food.

Anselm went to one of the two doors and tried to eavesdrop but no noise came from outside, nothing at all.

Then he tried to call Cyr in a tone high enough to reach an eventual room nearby but no answer was heard.

The knight made a second attempt but it was vain too.

After some time spent rummaging inside drawers and furniture inside the room, he found that there was no tool by which to try to escape, therefore he resigned himself to the idea of being locked up in there and, having nothing better to do, he decided to scan the landscape outside the half-open window: he also saw the back of the building and was enchanted for a few minutes to contemplate the green sea that swayed above the walls, the end of which could not be seen.

He was then distracted by a bird that perched on the top of one of the towers and stood there for a few minutes to observe the castle; what seemed to him to be a sort of pigeon was watching him moving his head left and right, until, suddenly, it flew up and headed somewhere towards the castle, disappearing from sight.

While he was absorbed in his thoughts, someone was trying to open the door in front of the window and, a few moments later, Kellar, Bryce, two guards and Evelune entered.

Immediately the woman ran towards Anselm and the two embraced again.

"So, what did you decide?" Bryce said turning to the knight

"I want you to leave us alone!" he replied

"Anselm...they told me that if you don't go to the Reginald's castle, they will keep me here forever locked in the room where I am now...and I wouldn't even know your fate" the woman intervened sobbing slightly.

"I may not be able to see you again, Evelune" he said taking her hand

"But...at least we have a light of hope...in the other case, not even that..." she replied

"Maybe you're right" he continued, lowering his head

"You can try at least..."

"Let me see where you keep her" the knight told them

"It's not a matter for you" the owner of the building replied

"Granted! I'll go there...but if you hurt her..." Anselm replied

"You have chosen the wisest thing, you will see that everything will be right...and in the end you will be able to return home safely" Kellar replied giving a message of hope to the two.

"Where's Cyr?" the knight asked

"He's fine, and you'll see him before leaving" the other reassured him.

The next morning Anselm woke up very early and took the opportunity to get dressed and take a look out the window: the moon was still clearly visible in the clear sky of that day and a light fresh breeze was blowing from the north, making some large hawks circling to the ascending currents and then descending again, all tracing imaginary circles that intersected in various points.

In the distance, an old crow had perched on the top of a tree and enjoyed the rocking of the branch that made up and down because of the wind, not caring at all about the hawks that above him kept an eye on the landscape below waiting for some possible prey.

Some voices from the corridor distracted his thought that yielded to the vastness of the surrounding nature and brought him back to far worse reality; it was Bryce himself who entered and, inviting him to join him in the rooms on the lower floor, left him in the hands of the same two guards.

Once on the first floor, the knight was accompanied to the largest room of the manor where, sitting in front of the large table, his friend was already present, alone and disconsolate.

"Hey, Cyr! It's nice to see you again"

"Anselm! I was afraid you had already left..." the dwarf replied

"I was forced...Evelune wants me to go, otherwise she fears that they will divide us forever"

"What do you mean?"

"They'll keep her prisoner in here...and if I didn't come back or even worse, if I tried to cheat them in any way, they'll kill her"

"We will find justice later...in any case I will try to help you in every way"

"Thank you very much, my friend"

"I hope you have spent a pleasant night in our home" the voice of Eustace, who entered with a hurried step, exclaimed

The two looked at him and just nodded.

Shortly after Bryce entered with a rolled-up paper in his hand which he placed on the table and showed the knight.

The map showed the way to go from the Intricate Wood to Elysande and had been reproduced in great detail by a hand skilled in the drawing and certainly knowledgeable of the place: marshy soils, streams with their fords, small woods were indicated, abandoned shacks, forgotten ravines and even a gorge where large packs of wolves were present.

In the lower part of the map, on the right, there was a rocky plateau, above which there was an "X", and next to the letter there was the writing "Elysande".

"There is everything you need to know about your trip...pay close attention to the wolves of the Echo's Valley, they are very aggressive and anyone who passes by hardly gets out of it alive! In fact, if I can give you some advice as a friend, avoid that place" Bryce exclaimed

"Cyr will come with me" Anselm said, ignoring what the counselor was saying to him

"He can't help you" the other replied

"Why? I'm here on purpose!" the dwarf intervened proudly

"They are orders from Kellar"

"You can't stop him from coming with me" Anselm continued

"Do you think they don't notice him? Do you ever see a dwarf around here?"

"I will somehow get in...you have to let me go with him!" Cyr replied

"These are topics that I have already discussed with Kellar...you can't enter his fortress except from the main entrance, and they would never allow a dwarf to enter, so the mission should not be put at risk...I don't have time to discuss further on this thing"

Eustace stood up and, before leaving, urged the knight to leave to get ahead.

So Anselm prepared his things, making sure that there was no shortage of water, a good dose of biscuits, Reginald's guards uniform, the map and his sword, greeted Cyr, gave a last goodbye to Evelune who was waiting for him outside the palace, giving her a kiss and promising her that he would be back soon to free her, and he left for Elysande on his horse.

V

Inside the Intricate Wood, Anselm was escorted by two guards on horseback who helped him to cover the shortest stretch avoiding other traps, accompanying him to the southern reaches of the forest.

There he went out and finally returned to see the infinite sky again.

The wild nature of that place was so evident that wild animals were visible everywhere and, at the passage of the knight, they ran to hide frightened behind some small rocks or under some holes dug in the ground, and everywhere you could see traces of animals, ranging from foxes to wild boar, from squirrels to big deer.

The soil was covered by a layer of not very high grass, and wild trees grew spontaneous everywhere, scattered here and there, giving a little shade to anyone who traveled those plains under the summer heat.

Aster was galloping at full speed and Anselm intended to reach his destination in no more than two days, therefore he had persuaded himself to spend only one night around those wastelands.

The Plain of the Wind was so called because this flat grassy expanse was beaten by a perennial wind from the north-east that, at times, was of such intensity that it shook some large trees so much that their trunks collapsed on the ground breaking; it was an inhospitable territory for humans but it was still the best way of communication, since the alternative was to cross the snowy mountain ranges that surrounded it.

After a few hours of travel, the surrounding environment began to change, and endless flower fields full of many colours began to appear, ranging from red to yellow, to deep blue, and the grass was much higher; even the trees were more numerous and occasionally roe deer appeared suddenly so, at the sight of the man on horseback, they made long leaps in the air until they quickly disappear behind the vegetation.

Anselm's gaze was suddenly drawn by an object in the distance that protruded from the ground and which in no way seemed to be a kind of tree.

As he got closer and closer, in fact, the object took shape and turned out to be an old wooden dwelling with a pitched roof on which stood a metal griffin-shaped wind vane that made a squeaking noise whenever it moved due to the wind.

When the knight arrived a few meters from the cottage, he saw a woman in a long white dress, intent on washing clothes in the well just in front of the entrance.

Anselm greeted the woman with great courtesy and she, surprised by his unexpected presence, remained silent for a few moments to observe him, but then greeted him with great kindness, also giving him a smile.

She was a slim, small woman with very long black hair that she kept tied with a string, and with a character that seemed to be very affable.

"Hello! My name is Isolde" the woman said, taking a few steps towards him

"And mine is Anselm! It is a pleasure to meet you"

"What reason drives you to come through these places?" she asked

"I have to go to Elysande"

"Uhm...I haven't heard of that remote place for a long time...do you live there?"

"No...well...I..."

"Oh, it doesn't matter...it was just my curiosity...I don't see many people passing by here..."

"Not even the knights of Reginald?"

"Well, here...sometimes I see some men in the distance on horseback but they almost always run like arrows over there, further west...and we do not distinguish them from here"

"So you don't live alone..."

"My husband is over there at the stream!"

"Ah...well, so I can freshen myself up" Anselm said with joy

"No...wait! Enter the house where I have fresh water and good freshly baked bread" Isolde continued

"I gladly accept your offer" the knight replied

"Very well, come in!"

Isolde hung out those few clothes on the clothes-line between two small fruit trees and entered the house, inviting the man to do the same.

It was a beautiful wooden cottage equipped with everything that was necessary to live and gave a really welcoming impression, especially on a summer day with the light of the sunshine that illuminated everything, instilling joy and life.

Isolde offered Anselm a mug full of fresh water and a few slices of bread which he seemed to like very much; in addition, the woman returned from the kitchen with fruit biscuits that were so appreciated by Anselm that they finished in the twinkling of an eye.

The front door opened wide and a gentleman of medium height, and with a long reddish beard that covered part of his check shirt he was wearing, entered in a great hurry.

"Hello!" Anselm said standing up and giving the man a smile

"who are you?" he replied with an astonished look, turning his eyes first towards the stranger then towards the woman

"I let him to come in because he was thirsty, Eluard" the woman intervened, going up to the slightly fatigued man

"My name is Anselm...and I'm from..."

"He has to go to Elysande" Isolde continued

"What are you going to do in that far away place?" he asked in amazement

"I have to run an errand for Kellar, the keeper of the palace in the Intricate Wood" Anselm replied

"Do you live in that place?" Eluard asked, looking at him with inquiring eyes

"no! I am from Thedra, the village north of the forest"

"I know those beautiful lands..."

"Eluard, I would need more water, what you took is not enough" Isolde intervened turning to her husband

"I'm going to get more"

"I will accompany you, so I will wash my head because I feel hot" Anselm said

"Well now, let's go! I'll show you the way...tell me a little about yourself" Eluard exclaimed

The two men went to the stream talking about advantages and disadvantages of life in those places and they were on very friendly terms; once they reached the site, they filled four containers with water and Anselm took the opportunity to rinse his face and legs.

The stream quickly flowed east and crossed the whole plain until it reached the rocky hills that ended abruptly on the edge of the precipice that bordered the Plain of the Wind.

"When are you going to get there?" the man asked the knight

"If all goes well, I should get there late tomorrow"

"And where would you sleep tonight?"

"At any place...where I can arrive" Anselm replied with a smile

"You can sleep with us tonight, we have a bed available"

"I do not want to disturb, I just wanted to freshen myself up"

"I advise you not to sleep outdoors in these lands, it is very dangerous because of the wild animals"

"Are you talking about wolves perhaps?"

"Exactly...at night they come out of the Valley of Echo to go hunting"

"Okay, you convinced me, Eluard"

"I'm happy...otherwise I would have you on my conscience" the man replied laughing

The two men continued in the speeches for half an hour until the distant voice of Isolde was heard calling her husband.

The sunset had come and the two eyes of the sky were both clearly visible: the one, more dazzling, was about to close hiding behind the horizon, the other, with its pale light, was wide-open to the maximum and showed itself more and more above in the sky.

Once back home, the three dined and spent the evening chatting and drinking good cherry juice mixed with mead, a delicacy that Anselm did not know but that, that evening, made him drunk so much that Eluard and Isolde were forced to drag him on the bed.

VI

Evelune was in the courtyard of the palace behind a small hedge at dead of night: a guard who was going to and fro in front of the large door, sat on the paving launching some yawns in the night silence and began to give in to the grip of sleep.

That night there weren't the two guards that were usually there or, at least, there was no trace of one of them.

The woman took advantage of the situation to run quickly towards the tower to the right of the manor and stealthily entered through the narrow door that led upwards through the wooden spiral stairs.

Going up silently, she reached the first floor of the tower where there was a window from which you could glimpse the sparkling moon, and taking a quick look outside, she saw a guard walking on the corridor of the walls and patrolling the external night landscape holding his long bow.

Evelune kept an eye on him for a few moments to see what movements he was making and, once the guard was moving away, she took the rope she had with her, tied it firmly to a rung of the ladder and threw it making it fall off the walls.

Making sure that it reached the ground, the woman came out of the opening grabbing the rope and slowly began to descend along the very high walls.

As she descended in the silent night, she heard the sound of the guard's footsteps approaching, so the woman stopped for a moment to make no noise, holding on to the rope with all the strength she had; hearing the footsteps of the man returning to go away, Evelune took courage and continued the descent.

Suddenly she put her foot on a wobbly protruding stone that came off from the walls and the woman, slipping, lost her balance and fell down...

"Nooo...!" Anselm shouted, waking up with a start.

He was all sweaty and, looking around, he saw, in the darkness of the room, the moonlight filtering through the window...it was just a bad dream, he thought.

VII

In Thedra, meanwhile, the villagers learned of Anselm and Evelune's disappearance since a friend of the latter, Clarice, had come to knock on their door the morning after the crime and, seeing neither of them at home, she warned a neighbour who then spread the news around the town.

At this news, a friend of the knight, Bernard, who was a blacksmith by trade, became very suspicious of this mysterious story and decided to investigate; arrived in front of his friend's house, he began to call and peer inside the various windows but, not hearing or seeing anyone, he took the nail remover he had brought with him and, with great ease, managed to open the front door.

Once inside, he noticed that inside there was nothing particularly strange except that there was a cup of coffee on the table that remained there, still full.

The man glanced around the hall and the other rooms but nothing struck him to alarm him.

For a moment he stopped in the kitchen and, looking at the external surroundings that could be seen from the window, he remained there thinking about what could have happened to the two.

"They have never left at night without warning anyone...he would have told me if he had gone somewhere" Bernard said to himself.

He did not know what to do and, in doubt, decided to get out of there to look for any traces outside the house.

Just when he was about to leave, Bernard immediately noticed the sheet of paper with the dagger still stuck in the door and felt a shiver of terror flow from his head to his feet.

When he read the writing he was pervaded by a sudden will to go immediately to the forest in search of the two but he knew, like everyone else, the great danger of that place so, after careful reflection, he chose to inform some of his friends of what had happened to recruit any travelling companions.

Bernard managed to convince only Faramond, his longtime friend and companion of Anselm's thousand adventures, so the two men left the next day for the Intricate Wood.

They entered the forest with a feeling of strong nervousness, mainly due to the fact that both had never entered inside and feared that the giant green monster would engulf them brutally.

Entering already several kilometers, the two continued with slow and cautious gait, trying to see some trace of human presence but, until that moment, the outcome was vain.

At a certain point, Faramond's horse tripped over something on the ground and, like a flash, some arrows started from a certain direction and one of them hit its rider on his left shoulder, injuring him and making him fall to the ground.

A cry of pain was heard within a few hundred meters and Bernard, getting off his horse, rushed to help his injured friend.

The dart had pierced his shoulder and had the arrowhead on the other side; Bernard grabbed the part of the dart behind his friend's back with both hands and, trying to distract the other, broke it with a very rapid gesture causing another scream of pain, much more intense than the previous one.

Immediately after, when Faramond seemed almost unconscious, Bernard finished the operation quickly extracting the arrow and tamponing the wound with a cloth that he had on the saddle of his horse.

They both stood there for a few long minutes, while some animals around watched them with curious eyes from their secret hiding places.

Suddenly there was a sound of footsteps on the leaves that seemed to come from a single direction, but immediately afterwards, this creaking was heard all around and in fact Bernard, looking around, saw a group of men armed with bows and crossbows approach, all dressed in dark green.

There were seven men on foot advancing at a quick pace and one of these, with a resolute tone, said:

"Don't move, you're surrounded"

"My friend is injured, he needs treatment" Bernard replied

"They'll take care of him at the palace! Come with us!" the same voice continued

Faramond was loaded onto his horse so they all went together in a direction unknown to the two men of Thedra.

After a long way, the group was in an avenue, the same one crossed by Anselm and Cyr, in fact shortly afterwards they were in front of an immense palace that stood in the middle of that green forest that seemed to be interminable.

The two were led inside the building and they waited in a large hall escorted by well-armed guards; a few moments later, Kellar came in and asked them who they were and where they came from.

Faramond, still suffering, replied:

"We are from Thedra...my name is Faramond"

"I'm Bernard and..."

"So you come from Thedra" Kellar repeated

"We were in the forest looking for a friend of ours" Bernard said

"And who is this friend of yours?" the master of the palace asked them

"Maybe you can know him" Faramond replied in a provocative tone

"I'd just have a surprise for you" Kellar replied

"Now I finally understand everything...here is revealed the truth about the danger of Intricate Forest" Bernard exclaimed

"You were very lucky, you could have done an unpleasant end inside there"

"Those damned arrows could have killed me if they had hit me a little closer to my chest" Faramond said

"I'm sorry but we had to do it"

"you had to?!?" Bernard exclaimed very annoyed

"It's a long story, I don't think you care about it..." Kellar replied

"Instead we care about it a lot!" Bernard continued

"That forest prevents us from going south to find new resources for Thedra" Faramond echoed

"You're right, it seems to me that you have the right to know"

Kellar told the facts to the two men and they listened to his words with great attention.

The owner of the palace also told them a precise episode in which some of his guards were passing through the Intricate Forest to escort his sister, Elaine, who was to go to Argalia, a town north of Thedra; during the way in the forest, the guards were attacked by a group of men, who had hidden on some large oak trees, and were massacred by them; after killing the guards, the assailants raped and killed poor Elaine as well.

When this massacre was discovered, the body of one of those men was found on the spot, wearing the clothes of Reginald's guards.

Upon hearing those words, Bernard and Faramond felt great anger towards the author of that massacre and showed, for a moment, understanding towards Kellar, but this did not however distract them from the current situation.

Just then, a door of the hall was opened wide and two armed men entered, followed by a very beautiful blond woman: it was Evelune!

The joy in the eyes of the two was great in seeing her still alive and both rushed towards her to greet her, when two other guards arrived from the same door, escorting a being much lower than themselves; Faramond and Bernard immediately recognized Cyr and, not having learned of his disappearance, they remained rather surprised and, being taken unawares by his presence, simply greeted him without asking him what he was doing there.

A few moments later Eustace and Bryce also entered together, so they all sat together around the large table.

"Well...I think we're all together now" Kellar said

"I wanted to inform you that all of you will remain guests in my building until your friend Anselm returns here and will help me find that spy..." he continued

"Where did Anselm go?" Faramond asked

"They blackmailed him!" Cyr abruptly intervened and, having got up, was blocked by Eustace

"It wasn't a blackmail...he chose what suits him best" Kellar continued

"it's not true! You're a liar!" Cyr exclaimed

"Calm down, Cyr" Evelune said, placing her hand on his shoulder

"Take him away! The dwarf seems to be too agitated!" Kellar exclaimed to the guards there

Cyr tried to rebel against those men but they had the best effortlessly and, once they crossed the door, there were choked cries of pain that chilled the blood to Evelune and the other two "guests".

"Sorry for the bad inconvenience, I hope something like this doesn't happen again" Kellar said breaking the awkward silence that had been created at the table

"You haven't told us yet where our friend is..." Faramond insisted

"He went to the town of Elysande" Bryce said

"He will be back soon, you will see...you just have to be patient, I know he is a great fighter and he will do very well" Kellar continued

"They could kill him! I will never see him again! " Evelune said bursting into tears

"They won't kill him because his task is only to find out a name!" the owner of the manor replied

"Why did you do this...he had nothing to do with that...I had to remain with him..." the desperate woman continued without stopping shedding tears

"You must not despair..." Kellar said, taking the woman's arm with his hand as if to caress her

"Come with me" he continued inviting the woman to get up

"Why can't we go back to our house?" Bernard asked

"What would happen if you tried to follow your friend up to Elysande and Reginald found out everything?" Kellar replied, encircling the woman's waist with his arm

Evelune left the room crying and was accompanied by Kellar to her room, and he tried to comfort her but in vain.

Kellar called Isemay, one of the young housekeepers who had the task of ordering the house, asking her to take care of Evelune and to provide everything she needed.

Faramond and Bernard were also led to two separate rooms, although the two, still shocked by what they had known a little earlier, were unable to fully understand the dramatic situation.

VIII

It was a lovely sunny morning with a pleasant temperature and the sun, peeking through the large window facing east, caressed Anselm's face, waking him from a deep sleep.

He looked around and the thought immediately turned to Evelune and then to his mission and while he was thinking about that, he heard noises coming from the kitchen of the pretty house.

Anselm got up and, quickly putting on the blue and silver robe that Reginald's guards wore, saw Eluard and Isolde preparing to go out and then asked them:

"where are you going?"

"good morning! Did you recover, Anselm?" the man said smiling

"Uhm...yes...good morning to both of you"

"I prepared something to eat for you" the woman said

"Thank you very much, you are very kind...but could I know where you are going?" Anselm asked again

"We have decided to accompany you!" the woman answered, adjusting her dark red cape

"But I have to go there alone...if they discover you and my mission fails..." the young knight said softly

"Don't worry Anselm...we won't come to Elysande with you, we'll accompany you until just before the town! I am sure we will be of great help to you!" Eluard answered

"We know those places" Isolde intervened

"They gave me this map..." the knight said showing it to the two

"If you need suddenly, I don't think you have time to look at it and to realize exactly where you are and in which direction you have to go..." Eluard exclaimed

"It seems a wise consideration" Anselm replied, patting him on the arm

"I'm going to prepare the horses" Eluard finally said before hurrying out of the house

"I am very pleased to have your company" the knight of Thedra said

"We are pleased too...and I am particularly happy because almost no one ever stops in these lands: many men on horseback pass by, far away, without ever stopping and having a chat" Isolde declared, showing all her joy

"Well...I think it's time to go, don't you think?"

"Yes, you're right...I'm ready!" the woman said, grabbing the crossbow that Eluard had given her

Anselm even forgot to eat because of the anxiety of leaving and, having got ready, went out to go towards the small stable where Eluard was waiting for them.

The horses were ready and Aster, at the sight of his jockey, raised its muzzle and emitted a neigh that spread in the air.

The three left at a gallop in the vast prairie, leaving behind that house which was now only a distant dark dot in the middle of the greenery; Aster led the trio although Isolde's horse was very fast and strong, while Eluard stood behind taking advantage of the their wake.

After some time, the three horses slowed down their run and Eluard decided to stop for a few moments at a small stream that was nearby to water the animals and to cool them down.

The wonderful water was so clear that, when Anselm bent down to wet his face, he saw his reflected image that moved in a continuous sway, and this vision enchanted him for a few seconds until, next to that face floating, another one equally changeable appeared and seemed to smile at him.

"It's called Bluevein" Isolde said smiling

"Sorry, what?...I don't understand..." Anselm asked

"I meant the stream..."

"It's very beautiful, it reminds me of the one near my house"

"At the bottom, over there, it collides on some rocks and forms small waterfalls where it is very pleasant to swim" the woman said

"Do you remember that winter day, when we went there and it was totally frozen?" Eluard asked

"Who could forget it? There was a layer of ice that was twice as thick as that of the palm of a hand and yet below it you could see fish swimming magnificently!" Isolde replied

"It would be very nice to go back, but now we don't have enough time" the man continued

"Yeah...It's better to set out again" the woman said

"Yes, I think it's time to leave" the knight concluded the speech.

So the three mounted again on horseback and set off again with an even more determined pace under the scorching sun of that splendid summer day.

After some time, Eluard shouted to his two travel companions inviting them to stop for a moment and look in the distance towards the southeast: it looked like an undefined dark mass that was approaching very quickly in their direction.

Anselm kept his right hand open resting on his forehead to cover himself from the sun rays which prevented him from seeing well, when, at a certain point, his eyes were able to distinguish very clearly that horde of knights who, flogging the ground, corrected their direction to go clearly towards the three of them.

Eluard was immediately alarmed and recognized the banner that one of those held in his hands.

"We have to go away from here as soon as possible! They are getting closer!" Anselm exclaimed nervously

"They are the knights of Reginald!" Eluard replied inciting his horse

"We cannot draw back, they will reach us" Isolde intervened

"Whoever talked about stepping back" the man replied

"Don't tell me..." the woman continued

"We are forced to go beyond there!" Eluard said pointing to his right

"That, if I mistake not, should be the Valley..." Anselm added

"Exactly...the Valley of Echo" the other continued

"But...there we risk..."

"Either we risk or we come to an end badly if we don't move!" Eluard said

"Let's move then, what are we waiting for?" Isolde replied

The three rode in a hurry to a path that descended abruptly and continued steeply towards a deep valley that separated the plain from the rocky mountains that rose above it; it was a ravine with lush vegetation where the sun rays, except when the sun was at its zenith, could not penetrate, so an immediate sensation of coolness pervaded the air above it.

Descending more and more, the three noticed the disturbing silence that reigned in that valley, where the continuous noise of the wind, that shook the trees and plants, was no longer heard, so much the less the singing of the various birds; it was as if this place was miles and miles away from the grassy plain where the three were until a few moments before and all this made it magical but at the same time gloomy.

When they had made a considerable way on that rugged steep path, Eluard stopped for a moment and, raising his head, scrutinized towards the top of that valley and he was able to see motionless human figures:

"Observe up there! It's them!"

"I don't see anything..." Anselm said

"Come over here" Isolde exclaimed

"Against the light...up there" Eluard pointed out

"Yes...now I see them! They stopped" Anselm exclaimed

"There is a reason so they did it..." Isolde said

Anselm looked into the woman's eyes and understood instantly.

"I think it's best to leave the horses here" Eluard said

"why?" Anselm asked

"I fear that we would not be able to take them with us, considering the place we will have to cross...we must find a shelter where to hide them"

"Will we come back to take them on return?" Isolde asked him

"Yes, but certainly we will not go back trough this valley"

Anselm saw that, about ten meters from them, a little higher, there was a ridge of rock that concealed a recess, also covered by a young beech tree that grew crooked as if to seek enough light beyond that shelter.

The horses were tied in that narrow natural refuge and Eluard provided them with enough fresh grass for at least some hours, after which the two men and the woman abandoned them continuing downward.

The figures on horseback placed on the ridge were still there to observe, until the three decided to continue the way penetrating into the belly of the valley so that they disappeared from their sight.

An increasing number of large beech trees with a whitish trunk and straight as poles were appearing to their eyes, and the thickening of the vegetation obviously proceeded at the same pace with the darkening of the surrounding environment, as well as with the clear-cut drop in temperature.

Those tall and straight trunks were rather disturbing because, under that vault of vegetation, you could glimpse the surrounding area even at a medium distance without however clearly distinguishing its depth and having an irrational feeling of being observed without being able to do it.

The silence that enveloped that place ceased when a slight sound of flowing water reached the ears of the three and in fact, just a little below, a stream was glimpsed among the dense bush, where it ran right at the lowest zone of that mysterious ravine.

It was called the River Jaws, since during the spring, after the melting of ice of the mountains, it swelled with water and engulfed part of the valley filling it up to flood the lower part of the beech trunks located in the lower part of the valley.

"We have to hurry before twilight comes" Eluard said

"You didn't tell me what you intend to do...here in the map it is indicated only the Valley of Echo, nothing else" Anselm said looking carefully at the map

"You absolutely must not go on this gorge...I will show you a passage that few people know!"

"well...where is it?" the knight asked

"It is located on the mountain ridge on the other side of the slope!"

"We came once a long time ago, I remember it as if it was yesterday...it's a very dangerous way" Isolde said

"Here we are at the river...we have to cross it, hurry up!"

"There is a small ford, come here!" Anselm exclaimed

He crossed the stream resting his feet on some boulders placed in a zigzag by someone and he was followed first by Isolde, then by Eluard.

As they walked up the other side through the beech wood, the neighing of a horse was heard echoing in the deep ravine and Anselm immediately recognized that animal.

"We will come back to take you, Aster!" the knight shouted

His scream rang in the valley as if it could not get out of that until it slowly disappeared into thin air.

"Do you understand now why it is called in this way?" the woman said to the knight

He smiled nodding to her.

After a few minutes, Eluard stopped abruptly, turning his gaze behind him and stared towards an indefinite point of the thick beech wood.

"What's wrong with you?" Isolde asked him

"I thought I heard something" he replied

Not hearing anything else, the man resumed the way and so the other two did the same but, as soon as they turned, that noise happened again and this time, behind them, there were not only the white trunks of the beech trees, but there was also a big dark grey wolf slowly advancing gritting its long teeth.

Although great was the terror that took hold of all three, Anselm unsheathed Aglet and stood in front of the other two with the sword held in both hands and turned upwards to strike terror into that ferocious beast.

The wolf did not hesitate yet and, as quick as a flash of lightning, threw itself with a long leap against Anselm; suddenly, while the animal made its assault, three other wolves of the same size emerged from the sides and simultaneously hurled themselves against Eluard and Isolde.

Anselm managed to hit the first wolf with a violent thrust and it was thrown to the ground a few meters from there, without however being able to prevent the wild animal from biting him on the left arm, injuring him not seriously.

In the meantime, Isolde managed to hit one of the three wolves with a dart of her crossbow, so that it fell dying to the ground, while Eluard collided with another wolf, ending up on the ground and fighting with it, trying to hit it with his sword.

The fourth wolf pounced on Isolde who was bitten in one leg and the woman lost consciousness for a few moments while the animal continued to rage on her; Anselm rushed against the wolf and hit it with the blade on its flank, killing it.

The last wolf, which was still fighting against Eluard, managed to injure the man by biting him several times on the whole body but in the end, with the help of the knight who intervened suddenly before it was too late, the two managed to overcome the ferocious animal.

The blood was everywhere, scattered on the ground, and, among the three, Isolde undoubtedly got the worst of it, in fact she remained motionless on the ground in a state of semi-unconsciousness.

Anselm stood up painfully to make sure his two friends were still alive but he realized that both were seriously injured.

Then the knight decided to pour some water on the wounds of the other two and this meant that Eluard raised his head to look and thank his friend, while Isolde barely managed to emit a groan of pain.

Anselm stopped the haemorrhage of the blood, especially from the wound in Isolde's leg, and cleaned the wounds by covering them with tufts of fresh grass put under a few pieces of cloth.

Finally he gave them water to drink and this seemed the thing that most regenerated them, at least there and then.

After a few minutes, Eluard struggled to succeed to stand up and stooped on his woman, caressing her face; Isolde opened her eyes and smiled at him despite the pain.

"We have to get out of here before other wolves come" he said painfully

"We won't be able to repel another attack from these beasts" Anselm said

"Can you stand up?" Eluard said turning to the woman

"Help me..." she replied

The two men helped Isolde to stand up and, although with great effort and caution, she was able to do it and take a few steps.

"You are not obliged to accompany me, you have already done me many favours" Anselm said to them

"Now we should go on, the passage is not so far from here" Eluard replied touching the wound that caused him the most pain

"Let's get away, hurry up!" Isolde said limping.

The three went up the northern side of the valley trying to do as quickly as possible and thus avoid that the other wolves of that pack reached them.

It was very demanding to climb that steep slope with the wounds that caused pain at intervals very intense and, moreover, with the anguish that at any moment those beasts could appear suddenly behind them.

What gave them the strength to go on was the fear that a scene like the one they had just experienced would repeat again, so the three continued with great determination and so much adrenaline in their bodies.

The sun began its slow descent towards the west and, although inside the deep ravine its atmospheric effects were quite attenuated, the situation was visibly worsening, with the temperature falling and, above all, the brightness decreasing more and more, and this was a grave situation.

A few tens of meters from their destination, a loud howl echoed in the valley and it literally gave the three the shivers, but the most chilling thing was that these initial howls coming from a certain direction of the ravine were followed by a series of other howls of packs of wolves that were located elsewhere, and they seemed to be hundreds and hundreds.

Anselm helped Isolde to speed up the pace because he feared the worst and, with great relief, the three finally reached the point where the rocks allowed to climb towards the passage through the mountain.

Isolde started the climb first, followed by Eluard and finally by Anselm who, meanwhile, controlled the situation below him; using protruding stones that greatly facilitated the scramble, the woman arrived with great joy on the rocky surface that indicated the beginning of the track and, exhausted from fatigue and pain, collapsed on the way.

Soon after, Eluard joined her and, having made sure the presence of his friend below him, he stretched out beside the woman to rest and cheer her up a bit.

Turning his gaze to his right, Eluard saw Anselm's hand grasp the edge of the rock and so he gave him a hand to help him climb; just when the knight had managed to reach the secret way, the growl and howl of some wolves could be heard very well below him.

Anselm leaned over the edge of the rock to observe the scene below and saw, with great disturbance, about thirty black-coloured wolves snarling upwards showing sharp teeth like knives and eyes that seemed possessed.

"We had a narrow escape..." Anselm said

"I was afraid I wouldn't get away with it" Eluard replied

"We have to thank you...you saved our lives, Anselm" Isolde whispered

"I did what you would have done for me...if you just leaned over, you would realize how many wolves there are below, it's incredible..." the knight said resting his head on the rock in exhaustion.

IX

After resting for a few minutes, Eluard checked the wounds and the expression of pain on his face was a clear answer to Anselm who was looking at him to know how he was; soon after, Isolde got up and seemed to have regained her strength even if she continued to limp in a visible way.

Eluard could not resist the temptation to look below them: from above, it seemed impossible that they had passed from there because that wall was about ten meters high and when he saw all those angry beasts down there, he withdrew his head drawing back.

The three decided to leave and set off on that rocky path suspended over the void.

After a few hundred meters, Eluard, who led the group, warned the other two to be careful as the passage narrowed to a width of just over half a meter and, in order not to risk falling into the precipice, the three continued ahead feeling the rock to keep safe.

Isolde took a quick look behind her and, seeing that the height of the precipice had significantly increased, she stiffened and had a dizziness; Eluard noticed that something was wrong and asked her:

"Hey...is everything all right?"

"Yes, sorry...I suffer a little dizziness" she replied reassuring him

"Don't look down!"

"When does this cursed path end?" Anselm asked

"Soon the worst part of it begins, my friend...so be very careful!"

"I guess not so many people have passed here" the knight continued

"You are walking on the Rock of Grin...do you know it?"

"I've never heard of him...who is this man?"

"Grin was a dwarf, but not just any dwarf...he was the king of the dwarves inside the mountain, the one you are now touching with your hands" Eluard said

"A dwarf? Tell me more "

"Dwarves are said to be excellent miners...I don't know if they are only legends or not, the fact is that one day a dwarf from the distant lands of the south heard about huge quantities of copper mines inside this mountain and so he decided to come here and create a passage that would lead to the heart of the mountain; he was helped by many inhabitants of his village who, in a short time, scratched the mountain to create what we are now walking on...and so it got its name from its creator, who was, in fact, Grin"

"I have a friend who belongs to that breed" Anselm said

"I've never seen one, I thought they didn't exist" the other replied

"His name is Cyr...he comes from the southern lands"

"And...how did you know him?" Isolde intervened

"He came to settle in Thedra long time ago" Anselm replied

"So, as you said, there should be quarries here" the knight continued

"Exactly, you will see them soon indeed! Attention now! The passage is very narrow here!"

The path had become so narrow that it was barely enough to rest your foot along its width and the three clung to the rock as if they were to embrace it, without daring to look behind.

They went on this way for some tens of meters when, suddenly, a few steps from them, the rocky wall of the mountain seemed to block the passage.

A sense of bewilderment struck Anselm who looked first upwards and then below him, noting that they were higher and higher as well as without an escape route.

Eluard began to feel the rock in front of him at a specific point, when, suddenly, with great amazement of Anselm, he found a large stone slab which he moved easily until an access to a secret passage was discovered.

The tunnel had actually been dug so as to have a height suitable for a dwarf or a man of short stature, in fact, when the three entered, they had to slightly lower their heads in order to continue.

The secret corridor continued for about twenty meters inside the mountain and then deviated to the right; the light was barely perceptible and the three went on almost groping so as not to run into obstacles or holes when, suddenly, in front of them, the rock widened to become a real immense cave where some gleams of sun rays penetrated through side holes dug into the mountain.

It was the mine of the king of the dwarves, or at least this place was called in that way, and it was a large former copper quarry of which nothing seemed to be left but some small nocturnal animal that lived there undisturbed.

The mine had a more or less circular shape although it had irregularities on its surface and its maximum width was about fifteen meters, while, as regards the height, it even reached five meters.

On the opposite side to the one they had entered, there was another opening that was slightly wider than the other and so the three entered it continuing the path in semi-darkness.

That tunnel was much longer than the previous one and its end couldn't be seen, as no glimmer of light came from outside.

After a way that seemed interminable, the three found themselves in front of a crossroads and, having to choose, they turned to the right thinking that it, being facing the mountain side, finally led outside.

The corridor continued for about thirty meters after which it led to another cave, smaller than the previous one and very different from it;

the dim light that filtered from the outside through holes dug into the rock still managed to illuminate the room sufficiently to show what it kept inside: in the center of it there was a sort of stone table on which a rolled up rope was placed.

On one side of that kind of cave there were some very rudimentary axes and on the side, next to the wall, there was a trunk of solid wood closed by a metal padlock.

Anselm was immediately seized by the desire to find out what was inside that jewel-case, so he grabbed one of those axes and began to hit the padlock hard; shortly after it was broken away from the trunk and the knight opened it with great curiosity.

What Anselm, Eluard and Isolde expected to see was not undoubtedly what was in there, in fact the casket concealed a still shining metal battle ax that must have belonged to some warrior.

The knight decided to take it with him and, after closing the trunk, took a look around that cave, followed by Eluard and Isolde.

As they didn't find anything else of interest, the three came out of that mysterious place and went back to the previous road fork; from here, they walked into the other tunnel and, after a long way of sudden detours and long corridors full of humidity, they discerned a glimpse in the distance.

This time the light became more and more intense as they approached until the three saw a crack in the rock and finally found themselves outside the great mountain seeing the sky again.

The weather had changed, in fact a thin layer of whitish clouds had partially covered the sky, but without concealing the sun that was instead hiding behind the horizon.

It was a great relief to be back in the open air and the pleasure coming from the feeling of freedom made them forget about the painful wounds they had in their bodies.

Once they took a few steps beyond the exit and looked at the surrounding landscape, they realized that they had greatly shortened their journey and they spotted in the distance, a few hundred meters away, the presence of a village, perched on a rocky terrain delimited by high walls, which surrounded an imposing castle.

"Well, that's Elysande!" Eluard said pointing to that so impervious place

"Looking at it from here, it seems a very large town" Anselm replied

"Do you think you can accomplish your mission?" Isolde asked him, still suffering

"I have to do it, I have no other alternatives" Anselm replied preparing to leave

"I think our ways will divide here" the knight exclaimed

"We have to leave...we will come back to get the horses and you can come and get your Aster back when you want and when you can..." Eluard exclaimed taking Isolde's hands

Anselm nodded and, after greeting them and thanking them for all the help they gave him, left them heading for Elysande.

X

After he had crossed a long rocky slope, Anselm found himself on a sweet moor covered with extraordinary bright green lycopods that gave off an intense and pleasant smell.

The sun had disappeared from sight but its light still kept the darkness away and Anselm took advantage of it to speed up the pace and thus reach the town.

When, finally, the knight was near Elysande he hid behind some shrubs that sprouted like leopard spots and waited in silence keeping an eye on the situation.

The darkness enveloped everything and Anselm's thoughts went to Evelune, causing him a strong sense of depression; while he was waiting there, the sound of fast footsteps was heard a short distance away and Anselm, leaning over the vegetation to look, saw a small group of people in open order heading towards the entrance of the town.

Then the knight immediately took advantage of the right moment to join them hoping that his camouflage would let him go unnoticed.

Those men were actually Reginald's guards and wore flawless blue and silver uniforms that went down until the knees, just like the one he wore.

When the knight passed the walls and entered the village of Elysande, the moon was shining high in the sky and its glow shone through the moving clouds that seemed to have fun showing it and then hiding it again, in an infinite night game.

Elysande was a splendid town full of inns, blacksmiths, carpenters, with a large market where goods of all kinds were exchanged and, even at night, it was always full of life.

Anselm, following those guards like a hound does with game, also entered the large entrance door of the castle and, when he saw the guards going towards the upper rooms through long and narrow corridors, he was disoriented and thought that if he had to return to the front door, he would certainly have been lost in that labyrinth.

The castle was not very guarded inside and this surprised the knight greatly.

Each guard went inside his own personal room, all located on the third storey, along a large corridor that overlooked the manor's internal courtyard; Anselm saw that there were many rooms and waited for all of them to enter their rooms, so that he approached the door of one of those where no guard had entered and eavesdropped in silence for a few minutes.

The knight of Thedra did not hear any kind of noise, even if barely audible, therefore, with great caution, he opened the door and, spontaneously in order to avoid any problems, entered inside.

The room was empty and quite large, and Anselm noticed that it was also well furnished, although he didn't care so much about it in that moment because the only thing he was looking for was a bed to sleep on.

Having ascertained the security of that room, the knight locked the door and, after resting Aglet on the trunk beside the bed, he finally laid himself down on it and in a few minutes he collapsed into a deep sleep.

At the first sun rays that entered the room through the window, Anselm opened his eyes and, thinking of where he was, he seemed to have slept an eternity; it was eight in the morning and various voices and noises could be heard from the room coming from the castle but also from the outside surroundings.

Anselm opened the door and, once he made sure that nobody was there, grabbed Aglet and left the room, locking the door and taking the key with him.

He passed the entire corridor and went up the stairs that were at the end of it, reaching the upper floor of the castle; when he found himself in another corridor from the spiral staircase, he came across a guard who greeted him with a nod, and he returned in the same way without being noticed too much.

Turning to see if that guard was looking at him, Anselm said to himself:

"Damn! How stupid...I have to act as if nothing has happened...I'm a guard of Reginald"

While he was intent on this thought, at the end of that corridor, an armed guard appeared with a very tall and medium-sized man at his side, with a red robe that covered him entirely.

Anselm was very agitated and began to sweat but he tried as much as possible to go straight and prepare something to invent for the moment, when that man in red called him:

"Hey! Come with me!"

Anselm nodded yes and followed that man keeping the same distance of the other guard.

The three went down the stairs to the first floor of the majestic manor and, once they entered a large hall with a very long table, two fireplaces on two opposite sides and a large bookcase at the bottom, the same man dressed in red invited the guards present there to sit.

Anselm sat down when, suddenly, his gaze focused on the center of that long table in front of him; in the middle there was an inlay work on the wood that represented a tree with seven branches and he immediately thought of that wooden chair he had in his home: the tree was exactly identical!

Anselm's mind completely estranged and he wondered who his father was, what he had to do with Reginald and what that symbol meant.

While he was concentrated in these thoughts, a voice broke the silence:

"This morning I received news that the squad of knights led by Marion that I have just sent north will be attacked by the men of Kellar, in fact they intend to kidnap her using her as a ransom...you absolutely must reach them before they arrive in the forest and tell them to go back"

"We will leave immediately" Adelard, the chief of the king's guards, replied

"You, Adelard, will stay here with two guards to expedite a matter...four of you will have to leave now"

"So let's not waste any more time" Adelard replied

Then he ordered four guards, who were there in the great hall, to leave immediately and Anselm, who was not called for this task, was commissioned by Reginald, the man in the red suit, to go to the highest tower and warn him when he saw his wife Marion returning.

Anselm immediately carried out the order and walked towards the corridor and then climbed the stairs to the upper floor of the castle, while his mind was absorbed in that mystery linked to that symbol.

Once up there, he began to look for the access to the tower with great circumspection, although luck was on his side, in fact there was no one else but him in that moment.

Anselm checked every room that was on that floor until he reached the last door on the bottom on the right, smaller than the others.

When he opened it, he saw a spiral staircase in front of him and decided to climb even higher until, when he reached the top, he found himself on a landing on which there was a small wooden staircase that reached the ceiling.

Once the knight raised the heavy trap door, a draught of fresh air caressed his face and Anselm finally reached the top of the highest tower of the Reginald's castle, from which you could observe anything that happened within a radius of a few kilometers.

Up there, Anselm's gaze was drawn to four men on horseback, who moved quickly along the moor in a northerly direction.

Thinking that he had enough time before those knights returned with the squad led by Marion, Anselm decided to go back down to the top storey of the manor and, going down the stairs of the tower, he began to have a look here and there.

While he was engaged in this action, he heard the sound of footsteps going up the corridor, followed by voices that whispered incomprehensible words at that distance.

Before you could say Jack Robinson, Anselm went back and hid just behind the door that led to the inside of the tower, waiting in a grave silence.

"This affair cannot go on forever"

"Yeah...but what can we do more?"

"We should team up with someone"

"Who will make a pact with us?"

"We could ask the peoples of the north for help"

"Our enemy is too strong, Reginald...we must avoid passing through that damned forest"

"And where do we go if we have to go north?"

"We can try to cross the great mountains"

"My dear Adelard...you also know very well that this suggestion is completely senseless...those mountains are impregnable, they have no passages and almost all the year they are covered by snow...there is no way to go through them"

"Then we have to come to terms with Kellar and stop waging war"

"He is the one who wages war against us! He's the one who wants dominion over that forest!"

"We must try to talk to him"

"No, Adelard! We have already done it and you know how it ended"

The two stopped and there was a moment of silence, then a voice started talking again:

"Kellar seems to have no weak points...he would be willing to get rid of anyone who put him in a difficult situation, even the people closest to him"

"Yeah, we know something about that..."

"That time he spread the news that the hired assassins of that massacre were my men"

"Unfortunately we have no evidence that the instigator of the murderers of his sister and his guards was him"

"We don't have them and we will never have them, it's true...but two things are certain: that man who was found there with the uniform of my guards was certainly not a man of mine and, as everyone knows, his sister was very critical towards him for the brutal methods he uses"

"All this is so creepy..."

"His sister was a good woman...she had great courage and also had natural virtues in the art of diplomacy"

"So what are you going to do, Reginald?"

"You can't deal with him, that's for sure"

While the two were discussing in a low voice, the sound of the creaking of a door did not escape their hearing.

"Go to the tower to see if they arrive"

"I'll be back immediately, Reginald"

When Anselm heard those words, his blood froze and, without delaying a second longer, he hurried up to climb the stairs until, having reached the top, he mounted the wooden ladder, opened the trap door and closed it quickly and furiously.

After a few moments the knight saw the trap door rise and Adelard's head came out.

"Do you see them coming back?"

"I still don't see anyone on the horizon" Anselm replied

"All right, as soon as you see something, let us know immediately" the other continued, peering north

Anselm nodded his head and so Adelard went back down to the upper floor of the castle where the king was waiting for him.

The knight of Thedra waited a few minutes after which he raised the trap door again and tried to make sure that the other was gone; no longer hearing any noise, he went back down inside the tower and, slowly, he came just behind the same door where he was before.

There were no voices or footsteps, so the knight came out from behind the door and looked out just to see if anyone was there.

The corridor was empty and it seemed that the two had evaporated so Anselm, in order to not to take any risks, went back to the top of the tower to wait.

The call of a bird that was wandering over the walls, in a westerly direction, distracted him from attention and Anselm, observing it, had the impression of having already seen it at the fortress of Kellar, in fact in those places it was very rare to see birds that they were not crows, eagles or hawks.

Suddenly, in the distance, Anselm glimpsed in that immense green heath a dark spot that approached the castle and, without even making sure that they were the four knights of Reginald, rushed downstairs to warn the king.

"Reginald! Reginald! " the young knight shouted

Reginald and Adelard came out of the last room at the end of the corridor and quickly ran so the three of them went up on the tower.

A group of about twenty riders galloped about two hundred meters from Elysande and the king recognized them without hesitation:

"They're really them...let's go down soon!"

Reginald, Anselm and Adelard went to the entrance of the castle to welcome them and, once inside, Marion greeted the king and led the guards on horseback towards the interior of the palace.

Everyone found themselves in the same large hall and Anselm, who was beginning to be at his ease, followed some guards who accompanied the king and the queen to their private rooms.

Reginald went to his private room with Marion and they began to argue, while the guards returned to the lower storey to receive orders from Adelard.

Anselm was entrusted with the task of supervising the upper floor of the manor and he considered himself lucky for what he had a mind to do.

XI

"If you weren't there, at this time I could have died" Marion said

"Luckily I received the message in time" Reginald replied

"They reached us a few hundred meters from the Intricate Wood...if we had gone faster, it would have been too late"

"Come on...don't be discouraged Marion" the king tried to cheer her up

"It's impossible to go on in this way" the woman exclaimed, putting her hands on her face in despair

There was a moment of silence in the room, so Anselm moved his ear away from the door and stood there in front of it waiting to understand if the two continued to argue or if they were going out.

When the two started talking again, the knight continued to eavesdrop but, suddenly, the guard who had the task of supervising the tower came out of it and saw Anselm who was listening in secret.

"Hey...what are you doing?" the guard shouted after a few seconds of waiting

Anselm was so taken by surprise that he said words stuttering conspicuously

"I was trying to...see if Reginald was here"

"I saw you stayed there for a while" the guard refuted loudly

Hearing talking outside the room, Reginald and Marion went out to see what was happening and immediately the king asked for explanations.

Anselm tried to defend himself but the guard directly accused him of wanting to spy on him and he was so much convincing in his speech that Reginald looked at Anselm and asked him why he was eavesdropping.

"Are you a spy sent by Kellar?" the king asked the knight

"I'm not a spy, Reginald" he replied

"So why were you secretly listening to what we said?" the king continued

Because of his non-answer, the king invited him to enter his room together with Marion and Adelard.

Feeling hunted down, Anselm decided to speak.

"I am not a spy but I was sent here by Kellar because I underwent a blackmail"

"Explain yourself better, we want to understand" Reginald said increasingly interested in the matter

"My name is Anselm and it all started when Evelune and I were out of our house enjoying the summer evening when, suddenly, we heard a noise a few meters from us and, seeing no one, I went to see what there was back there...I thought it was a wild animal but I didn't see anything or anyone so I waited for a moment to make sure that nobody was watching us or that some animal caught us by surprise. When I returned home there was no one, Evelune was gone! I found a sheet of paper that said that, in order to see her again, I had to go alone to the Intricate Wood and I went there! By chance, my friend Cyr, a dwarf from the southern lands, noticed all this, and so he followed me to the wood where we were captured by some men dressed in green..."

"They are Kellar's men" Reginald intervened, interrupting him

"Yeah...and those men led us to the fortress of Kellar where I finally saw Evelune again"

"And what did that killer want from you?" Marion asked with great curiosity

"He keeps her imprisoned in there until I fulfill this mission for him"

"What is it about?"

"He wants me to..."

"Come on, don't hesitate"

"He ordered me to come here and find out who was the Reginald's spy who lives in his palace"

Reginald smiled at Marion and continued:

"*She* has been living in there for a long time but she has always been very clever not to be discovered"

"So is it the truth?" Anselm asked

"Thanks to her we are able to know news that saved and that still saves the lives of many of us, including some wretches of the village who, ignoring the danger, would go into that wood"

"Kellar told me unpleasant things about the king of Elysande..."

"And what did he tell you?"

"That is a ruthless king who killed many people"

"Kellar is very good at telling lies..." Adelard intervened

"Yes...in fact he has been guilty of atrocious crimes! And all for longing for power! That man must be stopped at all costs" Marion continued

"He had his sister murdered!" the chief of the guards continued

Anselm made a disgusted and at the same time amazed expression with his face, pretending not to know this wrongdoing.

"Why would he have done such an action?" the knight asked

"He hated his sister...she did not listen to him and she did things her own way" Reginald said

"Okay...you convinced me" Anselm exclaimed

"But...wait...I don't quite understand what your place of origin is" the king said, fixing his gaze on the young man

"Uhm...forgive me, maybe I didn't say it...I'm from Thedra, north of the Intricate Wood"

"Thedra?" Reginald asked as if he had not understood that word well

"Exactly...do you know it well?"

"Uhm...yes..." the king replied

"can I ask you a question?" Anselm asked

"Provided that you don't ask me to reveal that name and then let you go" the king said laughing

"No...it's about a tree..."

"a tree? What is so interesting about a tree?" Reginald asked, catching great attention in the gaze of Marion and Adelard.

"That tree...I intend to refer to that symbol inlaid on the large table you have in your living room"

Reginald was confused for a moment, then started talking again:

"That is the coat of arms of Elysande: it represents the breadfruit tree and it symbolizes life, because it pervades every narrowest corner of my kingdom"

"Well, you see...Reginald...that symbol is also on a wooden throne that I have in my home in Thedra" the knight continued

"What?" the king asked in wonder

"My father made it..."

"Your father? That table was made by a very good carpenter whom I had the honour of meeting and hosting for a long time in my castle...he lived here in the village"

Anselm was silent for a few seconds without managing to conceal his great amazement, then continued:

"I really think that man..."

"What's his name?" Reginald asked

"Uhm...he really was..."

"Did he die in combat?"

"My father Alfred was killed in mysterious circumstances" the knight said sadly

"I can't believe it...you are Alfred's son...I knew him very well, he was a great man"

"I never knew who took him away from me"

"I can't answer either, Anselm...I'm really sorry" the king replied

"It doesn't matter...I will always remember him because he gave me Aglet, the sword of the great Brom"

"You have to know that he has been of great help here and I will always remember him as a very good carpenter, as well as a great man"

"I didn't know he lived here in Elysande" the knight said, still incredulous

"It's amazing how small our world is, young Anselm"

"Yeah...but we have to go back to our speech..." the knight continued

"So now...what are you going to do?"

"What are you referring to?"

"I guess you want to know who our spy is"

"If I went to Kellar to tell him that name, they would immediately kill your spy...I think..." Anselm replied

"I really think so"

"Then it's better to act differently...and then I'm only interested in saving Evelune"

"So...how do you intend to resolve the question?"

"I don't know...but how do you manage to communicate with your spy?" the young knight asked with great interest

"Now I'll show you"

The king turned his gaze to Adelard and nodded to him, after which the chief of the guards went to the window and made a whistle so long and acute that the echo made it bounce back several times, bursting even in the rooms of the castle.

After a few moments a bird entered the king's room and perched on the back of a chair; it was a big grey-brown sparrow hawk and in its right paw it had a small roll of paper tied.

"Now I understand..." Anselm exclaimed in amazement

"It was trained by our best falconer...so much good that it could fly to the Intricate Wood even with its eyes closed...it flies only at night so as not to be discovered by the enemy" the king said

"It is fantastic"

"I introduce you Arod, our messenger sparrow hawk"

Anselm looked at it with great admiration until it, with a rapid flap of wings, fluttered out the window and disappeared into the sky.

"I thought I saw it outside the fortress of Kellar...I mean...I'm almost sure it was Arod" the knight continued

"So, we said..." the king replied smiling for what the young man had just said

"Uhm...I would say that communicating to your spy to escape from that cursed place is another thing to avoid...in this case, Evelune and Cyr could risk their life" Anselm continued

"You have said wise words"

"We should think of a strategy"

"I was thinking the same thing"

"Let's take a few days and then decide...what do you say, Reginald?"

"I think it's a great idea" the king concluded.

XII

"That youngster will be very disappointed" a voice which then turned into a big laugh said

"I really think so" another replied, grinning aloud

"He thinks I'll release her..."

"what do you want to do?"

"A kind lady of such beauty deserves much more"

"In fact I have never seen such a beautiful one in front of my eyes"

"That's true...I will win her hand by giving her everything, if necessary I will also use the strength to keep her"

"And what will you do with him?"

"You have to get rid of him"

"We will do whatever you order"

"I will never forget what his father did"

"What are you talking about?"

"He fought standing by the enemy losing his life for it...now I will charge his son for that"

At those words, she stole away from the door without making a minimum of noise, and went immediately to the lower floor.

"Mrs. Evelune" a female voice from outside the room said

Soon after the woman repeatedly knocked on the door and finally heard the sound of footsteps approaching silently.

"who are you?" Evelune asked in a sleepy voice

"I am Isemay, the housekeeper" the female voice said

"And what do you want from me?"

"I have the task of taking care of you"

"I don't need anything, thank you very much"

"I have to tidy up your room"

"Could you come later?"

"I have to tell you something important"

At those words, Evelune opened the door and saw the woman looking at her waiting to enter, trembling with the desire to speak to her.

"Come inside...please" Evelune said

"Thank you very much..." the other replied

"What do you have so important to tell me?"

"I have to reveal some things I have just heard from Kellar"

"Who are you? Why do you tell me these things?"

"Well...I...I'm not..."

"What are you saying? How do I know you're telling me the truth?"

"You have to trust me! I'm here on behalf of Reginald!"

"I don't understand anything anymore, I'm very confused..."

"I heard he would like to take you away from Anselm"

"What?"

"Yes...he said that...he would like you to be his woman...and I also heard that he wants Anselm to be killed"

"It is not possible! It can't be true" Evelune exclaimed

"And then I heard him say something about his father that I didn't understand well..."

"I don't want to stay here forever" Evelune said, bursting into tears

"Kellar was right about one thing only..."

"What do you mean?"

"You are a very beautiful woman"

"I really thank you, but...help me, please...get me out of here, Isemay"

"If I could, I would help you"

"Why can't you? Maybe you don't want"

"Are you distrusting me yet?"

"No, but I don't understand why you can't free me and get me out of this damned prison" Evelune said sobbing

"Listen to me...you are entrusted to me now, if I free you they will understand with certainty that it was me and therefore they will discover me...and this means that they will kill me"

"So let's go away both"

"I think it's impossible...if they didn't see me even only for an hour they would be alarmed and they would find out us immediately! And then how would we both manage to escape? It's absolutely impossible"

"There will also be a way to escape from this situation..."

"We could try to..."

"Tell me...don't hesitate"

"Reginald and I communicate through Arod"

"And who is this Arod?"

"Well...it's not a person...It's a sparrow hawk!"

"What? A bird?"

"Yeah...it's the fastest and safest way to communicate with him"

"It seems a great idea!"

"I will write to him what I have just told you and that he should not trust Kellar"

"Well...what are we waiting for?"

"Not now...Arod has to fly only at night...it would be too dangerous now"

"Then we'll wait tonight" Evelune said with a consoled heart.

The day was drawing to a close and the long arc of the solar cycle had come down to the horizon, flooding the earth with shadow.

When the night completely darkened the sky, Isemay, who was in her personal room, threw open the window to take a look outside.

It was a typically summer night, starry and illuminated by the glow of the full moon and sounds of nocturnal animals from the neighboring forest could be heard very well.

At a certain point, the woman saw a bird fluttering among the branches of the trees in the woods and which seemed to hold a small prey in its clutches, when another bird of prey, most likely a big owl, pounced on the other bird to contend for the precious booty and the two were engaged in a furious fight in the silence of the night.

A little further down, two patrolling guards noticed that and, if initially they just watched the scene, after a while they pulled darts from their quivers and threw some arrows upwards with their long bows.

One of these arrows struck one of the two birds that fell to the ground in the middle of the woods emitting very well understandable calls, while the other bird of prey flew away taking refuge among the leafy tops of the trees, and this was followed by the sound of laughter of the two men.

Isemay did not believe her eyes: she knew all too well the call of that bird just killed...It was Arod.

Sadness filled the heart of the woman who was now also taken by great anguish because she no longer knew how to communicate with Reginald.

In the early morning, the woman, after completing her daily household chores, went to Evelune's room and knocked on the door to enter.

When she saw Isemay entering, she immediately asked if she had done what she had to do, but the housekeeper did not reply.

"Come on...what are you waiting for? So what's wrong?" Evelune asked

"This night something that was not supposed to happen, happened"

"Tell me everything"

"They killed Arod"

"And how did it happen?"

"Pure chance...It was attacked by an owl which wanted to steal a prey that It had captured..."

"Did it die for this reason?"

"No, let me finish...afterwards two guards, hearing the noises of that clash in the air, started throwing darts hitting Arod to death"

"And now...how will we do it? Luck doesn't seem to be on our side" Evelune said discouraged

"We will have to rethink another plan"

"Would you be able to free one of the prisoners?"

"I only have the keys of your room, but...I could try"

"Who has got the keys of their rooms?"

"Eustace for sure...but also the chief of the surveillance guards"

"I would say to avoid the first one, too much dangerous"

"I agree...wait! I have an idea! We can free that dwarf...he will be able to get out of here much more easily" Isemay said

"Yes, great idea! Cyr is the right man for us, sorry...uhm...the right dwarf for us!" Evelune continued smiling

"I just have to be able to steal the key of his prison from the guard"

"Go now and see if, by chance, he keeps them in his room...before the nightfall" Evelune said

"Yes...I'm going now! You have to stay here and be careful!"

Isemay left the room and, having locked the door and taken a look around, headed for the guards' rooms.

When she was in front of their chief's room, the woman slowly tried to open the door and realized that it was not locked: inside there was no one, so Isemay began to rummage here and there with extreme rapidity and without leaving nothing in disorder.

At a certain point, inside a drawer of a small closet, he found a bunch of keys, and so the woman grabbed it and, leaving the room by stealth, went to the rooms of the three prisoners.

The woman met some of the guards who were going downstairs and she greeted them very politely, receiving an equally kind greeting from them.

After moving some vases along the corridor to pretend to clean them, the woman glanced around and, making sure of the absolute absence of someone, rushed to the door of Cyr's room, tried some keys to open it and, at the third attempt, saw that it turned inside the lock.

Isemay entered the room quickly and, when she saw the dwarf who was on his bed, she motioned to keep silence.

Cyr, completely taken unawares, said softly:

"Who are you?"

"We do not have much time! You have to get out of here, right now! Go to Reginald's castle and tell him about Anselm...tell him that Kellar's men killed Arod and that Kellar wants to kill Anselm and take his woman so that your friend has no reason to hide..."

"But...why are you doing this?" Cyr asked again amazed

"There is no time to waste now...if they find out me here, they will kill everyone! Hurry up!"

Cyr wasted no time and left the room.

"Come on! Go beyond! That door over there leads directly to the cellars of the manor...from there you can go out into the internal courtyard, but be careful! If they catch you, it's the end for everyone!" Isemay whispered in a hurry

"Okay...see you soon! Thanks again..." Cyr replied, heading quickly for the door at the end.

Isemay locked the door again and, sensing the moment of great tension, cautiously went back to the room of the guard, placing the keys exactly where they were before, after which she went out and went back for doing household chores in the rooms.

A few moments later, she informed Evelune of the successful escape of the dwarf and she, breathing a sigh of relief, embraced Isemay to thank her.

XIII

Cyr went down the stairs until he found himself in a large, very cool cellar where crates of food, drinks, wood and other kinds of things were crammed; he immediately went to the exit and once outside, he took a look around to understand exactly where he was.

He was in the rear part of the inner courtyard of the fortress and from there you could see the stables of the horses where some men were intent on giving them some hay and cleaning the stables.

Cyr leaned out from a low wall to scan the surrounding area better and noticed, about twenty meters from those stables, an access through the walls that led to the outside.

The dwarf kept an eye on all the guards and the movements they made, after which he chose the right moment and went very quickly to the stable and, once he reached that, he hid inside, behind piles of hay.

Two men were saddling some horses which were then tied to a fence in the stable waiting to be ridden.

After a few moments, in fact, a man came to the stables and, riding one of the ready horses, went to the rear exit of the courtyard and disappeared behind the walls; subsequently other two men arrived and they did the same following the first rider.

Cyr observed from the opening in the stable that the access through the walls was still open and in fact there were still horses ready outside, in addition to the fact that the two stable-boys continued to carry out their work without stopping.

The dwarf understood that this was the right moment to seize the opportunity and, before you can say Jack Robinson, he came out of the hiding place, untied the rope that kept the smaller horse tied to the others and, without hesitating a second, he galloped towards the exit.

Cyr incited the horse to run at most but this thing attracted the attention of two men who were approaching the stables.

"Ehi, you! That's my horse!" one of the two yelled

The guards on the walls noticed what was happening and raised the alarm but when a guard tried to block the gate at the exit, Cyr's horse anticipated that man slightly and managed to get out of the fortress' courtyard.

Shortly after, Kellar and his men came running, and they immediately ordered a dozen men on horseback to chase the fugitive and capture him.

Kellar was furious and immediately went inside the castle to understand what had happened; once he knew that the dwarf had left his room, he gathered all his guards and interrogated each of them to find out the truth.

Kellar punished the chief of his guards by removing him from his appointment and replacing him directly with Eustace who decided to double the vigilance inside the castle.

Meanwhile Cyr continued his escape galloping into the forest, pursued with determination by the ten men on horseback who were breathing down his neck.

Cyr's horse extricated itself from that tangle of trees very well and managed, at least initially, to detach its pursuers.

Cyr was completely ignorant of the direction he had taken but knew that the important thing was not to be caught by Kellar's men, even if he couldn't find a way to get rid of them.

His escape continued with frantic pace and then the dwarf took a quick look behind him sometimes, managing to catch a glimpse of those men who seemed hounds which were chasing a fox.

After a while, when the already rather faint sunlight inside the Intricate Wood seemed to decrease further, Cyr found himself in a small grassy clearing where he could then better control, for a moment, the number of men who were chasing him.

They had managed to gain ground and this made the race of the dwarf even more feverish so, once he returned to the Intricate Wood, he tried to increase his pace again.

Suddenly his horse emitted a loud whinny and began to slow down but, when it actually managed to stop, it was already too late: in fact, right there in front of their eyes, there was an immense very deep gorge that delimited the endless forest.

The horse barely managed to save itself, while Cyr was thrown forward ending up down the ravine.

Behind them the ten knights noticed that so they pulled the reins of their horses stopping in time a few meters from the abyss.

Once on the edge of the precipice, the men on horseback watched carefully towards the bottom of the valley, waiting there for a few minutes.

"He will have gone to pieces" one of them said

"It is the end he deserved" another replied

"Come on, let's get the horse back and go back to the castle..." a third man exclaimed

They thus returned to the fortress and informed Kellar of the incident, and he, although still very annoyed for what had happened in the palace, felt a visible satisfaction for that news.

Kellar called Eustace and ordered him to keep an eye on the guards and any other suspects who walked around the corridors of the manor, as well as placing a guard for each prisoner's room.

XIV

The oak's root that escaped from the ground had turned out to be a great luck and Cyr clung to it until he heard the men leave.

Climbing for about four meters on that rock, the dwarf returned to the surface and, after taking a look around to make sure that there was nobody there, he cleaned himself up with a sigh of relief; he looked down towards the end of the ravine and thinking on what had happened to him he thanked heaven that everything had gone well.

But now he had remained on foot and the path to Elysande would have been much longer, so the dwarf started running to try to make up for some of the lost time.

Cyr skirted the edge of the ravine so as not to get lost inside the Intricate Wood and to avoid further traps and this also gave him great motivation in continuing his way because of the fact that he could occasionally be distracted by the magnificent beauty of the landscape that could be admired from up there.

After a couple of hours of walking at a fast pace, the dwarf caught a glimpse of the end of the forest and this made him very happy because he did not love the woods too much and he was fed up of being surrounded by trees and only trees.

When the forest was already behind him, the dwarf found himself in a large green prairie where the grass was very lush and even reached his waist.

After a few hundred meters, Cyr saw some big rocky boulders that concealed a beautiful stream with fresh and clear waters, where the dwarf immediately decided to dip his head to refresh himself, taking advantage also to quench his thirst and relax as he had covered dozens of kilometers at a fast pace and without stopping.

Suddenly he saw the water become muddy so he stood up immediately and, approaching a rock, he peered towards the stream: two horses were drinking tens of meters further, towards the source, in complete solitude.

They could not be in the wild because they had saddles, halters and reins, so the dwarf decided to remain hidden behind it, waiting to see what happened.

"And...who are you?" a voice behind Cyr said

The dwarf was caught by surprise and, at the sight of a woman, he greeted her politely introducing himself:

"I'm Cyr and I'm from Thedra"

"Another who comes from there" the female voice continued

"I'm actually originating from the south..."

"But...what kind of...uhm...I mean..."

Cyr burst into laughter and said:

"Yes, I understand...you've never seen a dwarf!"

"Well...really...no"

"Are you also from Thedra? I've never seen you"

"No...I meant that..."

"Isolda, I was looking for you...but...who are you?" said the voice of a man who drew his sword from his sheath

"Lower that weapon, Eluard...I don't think he's here to hurt us" the woman said

"I'm Cyr...I'm going south to save a friend of mine"

"And who is this friend of yours?" Eluard asked with great curiosity

"His name is Anselm...he is a knight of Thedra"

"We already know him..." the woman said approaching the dwarf

"Did he pass by here by chance?" the dwarf asked

"Yes...he told us he has to carry out a task for Kellar" the man said

"Yeah...for the man who wants to kill him" the dwarf exclaimed angrily

"He did not tell us this thing...why does Kellar want to kill him?" she asked

"Kellar wants to take his revenge and wants his woman"

"That man is really ruthless...it is better not to deal with him" Eluard said

"It's the truth...but now, if you allow me, I have to leave you because I'm in a hurry" Cyr exclaimed

"Wait! Anselm has left his horse...take it so you will arrive earlier and you can bring it back to him!" the man said

"Okay...I accept gladly! I'm tired of running" the dwarf said

Isolde mounted Cyr on her horse and so the three headed for their home and, once they arrived, they consigned Aster to the dwarf who, after thanking them several times for their immense kindness, set off southwards riding at great speed.

After a few hours of way, the dwarf finally arrived near the city of Elysande and thus headed towards the entrance door along the western side of the walls.

When the guards saw him, they ordered him to stop and those ones on the town walls aimed their threatening bows, so Cyr stopped and dismounted from the horse, showing himself unarmed and with peaceful intentions.

At the sight of the dwarf, the guards did not believe their eyes and one of them approached him saying:

"Who are you? And what is the reason for your visit to Elysande?"

"My name is Cyr and I am here for talking directly to your king"

"Do you know our king personally?"

"I have to report to Reginald some very important information"

"What is it about? We have to know, otherwise we can't let you in"

"It's about Kellar..."

On hearing that name, one of the guards told another to go to the king and tell him about that visit so that the man hurried to go to Reginald.

In the meantime he was waiting outside, Cyr gave Aster some water and fresh grass so that it was able to regain the energy lost in the long journey.

After some time, that guard returned and gave the dwarf consent to enter so the gate was thrown open and Cyr was accompanied by two men to the interior of the royal palace.

Escorted to a large wooden door located in the center of a long corridor, Cyr entered what was a large hall and saw that various people were waiting for him; among these, the dwarf recognized his friend immediately and, with a very natural attitude, went towards him:

"Anselm! I'm so glad to see you again...but I didn't expect you to be here..."

"Me too, Cyr! I know what you mean...I wasn't expecting this pleasant visit either" the knight said

"In fact I'm here by a miracle...I risked dying" the dwarf exclaimed

"But...how did you manage to escape?"

"A woman freed me"

"A woman? Come on...let me introduce you to Reginald!"

Cyr approached the king and bowed but the king invited him to stand up and said to him:

"I am Reginald and I am very pleased to meet you personally...I know that you are a great friend of Anselm, so you are welcome and you will be treated with a great spirit of friendship by whoever is in this town"

"Thank you, Reginald! I am very honored by this privilege and I will try to return this spirit of cordiality to all of you"

"They told me you have information to give us" the king exclaimed

"Well, yes...I came for exactly this reason...so I was informed that the men of Kellar killed a certain...uhm...Arod...yes, I am sure that *he* is called in this way..."

"That's why *it* hasn't returned since yesterday...I hope they couldn't read the information I had given *it*..."

"Uhm...who are you talking about?" the dwarf asked without understanding anything

"It was my sparrow hawk...we managed to communicate directly by using it...who knows what has happened to it..." Reginald said to himself

"That woman also told me that Kellar wants to kill you, Anselm!"

"Does he want to kill me??" the knight repeated unconsciously

"Yes...but there is an equally disturbing fact that you must know...he wants to keep your woman for himself"

"I can't believe it..." Anselm whispered angrily

"It's the truth...*she* told me this thing!"

"Who is she?"

"He is referring to Isemay..." Reginald intervened

"Who is such a woman?" Anselm asked

"*That's* her..." the king replied

"She is yours..."

"You finally found out, Anselm!" Reginald said smiling

"A woman...I never would have thought about that"

"That's exactly the reason I chose her"

"He'll pay dearly for it...he tricked me" the knight whispered

"He's used to doing it" the king replied

"He wanted me to come back to him with *that name* so that he would then kill me, Isemay and stay with Evelune..." Anselm said, almost speaking to himself

"We won't let him, don't worry" Reginald exclaimed trying to cheer him up

"Damn...now I don't know what to do" Anselm said putting his hands in his hair

"There is one last thing I have to tell you, Anselm...unfortunately Kellar also captured Faramond and Bernard"

"What do they have to do with this affair...?"

"They were looking for you and the same fate happened to them"

"This is not what I needed" Anselm regretted

After Cyr was introduced to Marion and Adelard, the king exclaimed:

"Well...we are gathered here to establish a plan that will free us once and for all from Kellar who, after these last events, has made life impossible for all of us: last night I reflected on a possible strategy to be adopted and a great idea came to my mind...I thought that only *he* could help us"

"Explain yourself better, Reginald" Anselm said

"Of course...therefore, north of Dark Lake, at the foot of one of the peaks that form the Western Chain, lives...or maybe should live, a certain Athelor, a skilled lumberjack who entered the Intricate Wood many years ago and was then captured by Kellar's men who imprisoned him inside the fortress; it is said that, after some time, he managed to escape through a secret tunnel that led directly outside the manor, more precisely in the middle of the forest..."

"*He should live*"..."*it is said*"..."it seems more a legend than a story that really happened" Cyr said

"He himself told these things but then he went to live over there to hide and make the enemy lose his tracks" the king replied

"And what would you think to do, Reginald?" the dwarf asked

"I was thinking that the fortress of Kellar could be attacked but, at the same time, someone must penetrate inside it to free Isemay and the prisoners..."

"Through that tunnel?" Cyr asked incredulously

"It seems to me a feasible thing" the king replied

"But...why haven't you used it in the past?" Anselm intervened

"Uhm...it is a very good question...well...the problem is that if you want to go to that place, you have to cross the marshes of Gliness" Reginald replied

"I've already heard of it" the knight said

"They are very dangerous" Adelard intervened

"Nobody has managed to cross them until now, except Athelor...in fact nobody knows how he was able to do that" the king exclaimed

"Many of our men died in those cursed swamps!" Marion exclaimed

"There are large quick-sands that no one has ever managed to cross..."

"We could attempt the passage through the mountains" Cyr replied

"Those mountains are too high...if you stayed alive, it would take you days and days to pass them without then being sure of finding the home of Athelor...the most direct way is through the marshes..."

"It really seems an impenetrable place" the dwarf said to himself

"If it is useful to free Evelune, I will go to Athelor's house" Anselm exclaimed firmly

"I didn't have any other alternative ideas to this one" Reginald continued

"Don't worry...as you said, he was able to do it, so it's not impossible" the knight said

"Well...what are we waiting for, Anselm?" the dwarf asked

"I hope you aren't thinking...I'm going alone, Cyr!" the knight replied

"I'm sorry but this time I won't chase you...so let me go with you! Save me the trouble of looking for you!" the dwarf continued

"As you wish, my friend"

"Let's get ready"

"Will you leave immediately?" Marion asked

"Yes, we have no time to waste" the knight replied

"Hey...I need a weapon" Cyr said grumbling

"Haha...you're right, I'll get you a sword" the king replied

"No! Wait, Reginald...I have something for you here, Cyr" Anselm said

Anselm took the battle ax he had taken from the mine inside the mountains from a leather case and showed it to the dwarf.

Cyr looked at the weapon in deep silence with amazed eyes that became shiny after a few moments.

"I found it inside the dwarves' mine" the knight said

"This...this is...it's Grin's ax...I recognize it by the symbol that is here"

"We found it inside a case"

"I can't believe my eyes...nobody knew where it was kept" the dwarf exclaimed

"Take it...it's yours now"

Cyr was mad with joy and, thanking his friend, said to him:

"I also have something for you..."

"What are you talking about?"

"I brought you Aster back!"

"Did you know Isolde and Eluard?"

"Exactly...I met them along the way, where the stream flows hidden by the rocks before ending in the waterfall"

"I'm glad you met them...they are very good people...thank you very much, Cyr"

"Let's get back to our speech now" the dwarf said

"I will need some long ropes, at least twenty meters..." Anselm exclaimed looking at the king

"I'll get some right now" the king replied inviting Adelard to go and get them

"Is there anything else you need?" Reginald asked

"I think so...a good bow, I could need it"

"I'll get that too...how many days do you plan to spend around there?"

"I don't know...explain to me the reason of this question"

"In the meantime that you and Cyr try to find Athelor, I will prepare my men for battle, then I will gather as many knights and bowmen as possible and, once ready, we will leave for the Intricate Wood..."

"I understand what you mean...therefore...give me three days, then we will meet in the afternoon of the third day at the hills where Bluevein ends its course, so we will move from there together to find ourselves in the forest at night" the knight proposed

"It seems a good plan, Anselm"

"If we delay, send someone to find us"

"I don't even consider the hypothesis that you fail!"

Thus it was that Anselm and Cyr left with their horses to go to the marshes of Gliness.

XV

After almost a day of walking along the wide plain, the knight and the dwarf glimpsed in the distance the majestic peaks of the Western Chain and this, if on the one hand it cheered them for having already arrived nearby the swamp, on the other it aroused in them a feeling of fear for the presence of that harsh and hostile landscape in front of them.

At a distance of about two hundred meters from them there was an imposing secular oak tree which had been given the name of Big Shadowy and the two decided to rest for a while under its majestic branches.

They noticed that, on one side of the trunk, a ladder made of ropes and wooden rods went down almost to touch the ground and thus, looking upwards, the two saw that, among the highest branches of that gigantic oak, there was a wooden hut that extended over the entire area of the thick foliage.

Anselm was so intrigued by that particular home that he decided to climb the rudimentary stairs as quietly as possible.

While the knight continued the climb, Cyr watched him in silence, ready to intervene in case of danger but, contrary to what the latter expected, the threat did not come from above the oak but behind him; the dwarf, in fact, heard the hiss of an arrow a few centimeters from his ears and saw the dart sticking into the hard bark of Big Shadowy, so he threw himself on the ground launching a warning cry to his friend.

Anselm immediately interrupted the climb and, drawing his sword, he peered down through the branches but, seeing still nothing, he went down to the lower part of the trunk where, a few tens of meters from there, he saw a man dressed in black, running and pointing a bow at him: the latter threw another dart that grazed him, hitting the trunk and breaking in two pieces.

Once the stranger was a few meters away from Big Shadowy, he drew his sword and threw himself against the dwarf who was sheltering behind the oak; the thrust of the sword was avoided by the dwarf who bent down and tried to hit his assailant with his ax but the man dressed in black was equally skilled in avoiding Cyr's slash so that he managed to throw himself into a second attack by dropping at land the ax of the dwarf who, at that point, went away to escape the assault.

At that point, Anselm's timely intervention avoided the worst and he stood in front of the man in black, blocking him and inviting him to fight.

The stranger then threw himself against Anselm launching a violent attack which was blocked by Aglet, so the knight tried to respond to his assault but the other's as quick as lightning hand canceled his attempt and was able to launch a second assault on Anselm who, also in this case, parried the slash but stepped back in front of his opponent.

Stopping in front of each other, the two men looked at each other before resuming the clash, while Cyr observed from a distance the mastery of that man dressed in black.

Suddenly the stranger pounced on Anselm who had to defend himself again but, this time, he was very able to repel the opponent's blade by moving it away from his body, so that in an equally sudden gesture he aimed Aglet on the other's chest.

Anselm ordered the other to stop and surrender and the man dressed in black, having no alternative, dropped his sword on the ground.

"Can I have the honour of knowing at least your name?" the stranger said

"My name is Anselm...and I congratulate you on your skill in the art of the sword...if you were now kind enough to tell me who you are..."

"I'm Rolf and what you see above is my home..."

"We didn't want to hurt you...we are only here to rest in the shade" the dwarf intervened approaching the two men

"I had never seen one of your race...what's your name?" Rolf asked

"I'm Cyr and I'm happy to meet someone who beat me in combat" the dwarf replied

"What drives you around here?" the man asked

"We have to go to the Western Chain to find someone to help us" Anselm said

"Who are you talking about? Nobody lives over there..."

"A certain Athelor should live up there, do you know anything about him?" Cyr asked

"I've heard of him...to be honest, I think I've seen such a man come from there and wander around here several times, but I don't know if he was the man you are talking about...how do you intend to reach those places?"

"We will have to cross the marshes of Gliness" Anselm said

"You don't know what you're going to face..." Rolf exclaimed

"They've already warned us...we'll find a way to go beyond them" Cyr intervened

"I myself once tried to go beyond it and I was about to die" the man dressed in black continued

"We have some ropes" the dwarf said

"We also had them but they weren't enough...I know from experience"

"We will set great store by your advice"

"I think it's time for me to go up the tree" Rolf said with a nod, turned towards his hut

"We'll leave you to your household chores" Anselm replied

"If you want, you can stop here! I'll welcome you"

"We thank you very much but we are in a hurry" the knight exclaimed

"Well...I wish you a good day and a good continuation"

Anselm and Cyr said goodbye to Rolf and left that place to continue towards the swamp.

Soon the ground changed radically, so much so that the horses' hooves began to sink slightly into the earth causing them greater effort; a layer of wet mud covered with blades of sedge had replaced the solid soil that constituted the grassland present as far as the Big Shadowy and even the air had become heavier, full of moisture and apparently so oppressive.

The ground was increasingly clayey when the two decided to go a little further north where to leave the horses there and tie them to some beech trees present in that area.

Cyr and Anselm walked slowly, paying close attention to where they put their feet until, at a certain point, the knight rested his right foot but the clayey soil beneath him subsided completely and he lost his balance falling to the ground; realizing what was happening, the dwarf rushed immediately to help his friend who was literally sinking, so he grabbed Anselm's hands and tried to pull him out with all his strength but Cyr slipped and he could not find hold on the ground because it was too muddy.

Being faced with this difficult situation, the dwarf decided to take one of the ropes and, once Anselm grasped its end, he backed away a few meters until he reached a point where his feet sank less into the ground and from there he began to pull the rope.

Cyr struggled a lot to pull the rope and only after Anselm managed to help him using his own hands, the dwarf was able to completely extract his friend from those deadly quicksand.

After resting for the great effort they both made, the two realized they were covered in mud up to their necks and realized that the situation was going badly.

Cyr proposed to walk for a large part of the area bordering the Dark Lake in an attempt to find a passage but the search was vain because the two found themselves several times in front of immense expanses of impenetrable quicksand.

"How did Athelor go beyond these damned swamps?" the dwarf wondered with great skepticism

"I don't really know...but if what Rolf saw was him, it means that somehow he succeeded"

"I think he goes through the mountains"

"Look at them, Cyr..."

"Well...what do they have?"

"They are too high...it is almost impossible to go to and fro through those peaks"

"Then I don't know...I don't want to give myself up but in the current situation I can't find a solution"

"Let's try to see how wide these quicksand are"

"And how are you going to find out?"

"I think I've found a way..."

Anselm took his bow and tied some ropes to a dart and began to throw it around in the direction of the lake, gradually farther and farther to discover any areas where the ground was hard and therefore passable; every time the arrow fell into the clay, he pulled the rope and retrieved the dart and then made another attempt.

The knight went on like this for some time until finally he discovered a point where the quicksand did not seem to be as extensive as elsewhere and decided that this should be the area to move forward.

While Anselm stopped to think of a stratagem, Cyr decided to try to see if indeed at that point he could continue the way and so he began to explore the ground with his hands until it seemed to him that there was a kind of passage right in front of him.

Suddenly, perhaps taken by the euphoria of having found an access, the dwarf pushed on without taking too many precautions, when, in the twinkling of an eye, he found himself in the ground immersed in that mud that was engulfing him very slowly.

Cyr uttered a cry for help and, as soon as Anselm realized the serious danger the dwarf was in, the latter rushed to him, throwing him a rope and trying to get him out of there.

The weight of the dwarf had increased considerably and Anselm was in difficulty to extract him from the mud because he couldn't remain stable on the ground, so he was panic-stricken and looked around for help, but obviously there was no one...

Anselm saw their horses watching them a few tens of meters away, and then an idea came to his mind: he told Cyr to hold on a few seconds while he ran at full speed towards Aster and, a few meters from his horse, he stumbled and fell to the ground bumping his head against the trunk of a young beech.

Standing up immediately, he mounted his horse and, a few meters from the dwarf who was sinking more and more, he tied a rope around the animal's shoulder and, throwing the opposite end of that to his friend, he gave Aster strokes with the stirrups and it advanced with great power extracting the dwarf from the sludge, saving his life.

"You have to be more careful...I couldn't have done it alone"

"Sorry, Anselm...I thought I had found a way with hard earth"

"Maybe I have a solution..."

"No...you don't pass through here...just ahead the ground is clayey as elsewhere"

"I meant maybe I discovered the way"

"What are you going to do now?"

"A few minutes ago I stumbled there and I ended up against the trunk of a beech..."

"So what? What do you think to solve with that?"

"I had an idea...we can use the trunks of those beech trees to go to the other side of the swamp"

"Make yourself clear, Anselm!"

"We can use them as bridges...those trees will be about thirty meters high...we can tie two of them and..."

"Yup! It seems a great idea! Come on, let's do our best!"

The two went to that point where their horses were and, after choosing the two highest and straightest beeches and with the trunk not too large, they took in turns hitting the lower part of the trunks with the battle ax of the dwarf.

After a short time the beech trees collapsed and the two began to cut their branches until they got two long poles; subsequently the trunks were dragged with the help of the horses near the swamp and there they were tied together with ropes, passing them round the cut branches.

When the two got what they wanted, they began to push that very long trunk until they reached the area of hard earth where Anselm had thrown his arrow just before.

Once he made sure that the trunk supported him, Anselm decided to go ahead first and, walking in the muddy ground, he slowly began to sink until he was submerged by the slime up to his neck; he advanced holding firmly on to the trunk with his hands and, despite the slowness of the movements, he managed, after a few minutes, to reach the opposite end of the long pole until he emerged from the quicksand.

Cyr waited for Anselm to come out of there and then did the same thing done by his friend until he found himself by his side.

When they regained their strength a little, the two did the same thing to move further and further forward until they finally found themselves a few steps from the shore of Dark Lake.

Exhausted by fatigue, they collapsed on the ground in a deep sleep just when the sun was reaching the horizon.

XVI

The following morning Anselm and Cyr woke up with the sound of water going back and forth on the lake shore because of the fresh breeze that beat in that rather exposed area.

The waters of the wide lake were of such an intense blue that it was impossible to glimpse any fish or any other living creature that was just below the surface.

Anselm decided to dive into the waters of the Dark Lake to get rid of all the dry slime scattered throughout the body and, although Cyr feared those waters so apparently deep and at first was very reluctant, he managed to convince the dwarf to do the same.

The two came out of the water completely clean and walked north along the lake.

After a few hours of walking, the two found themselves surrounded by a wild nature in which the only visible living beings were some crows that hovered high in the sky.

To their right the initial peaks of the Western Chain rose high, while on the left the lake continued to keep them company with its sweet but disturbing constant noise.

Entering in the middle of the high mountains' peaks, the two saw the end of the northern coast of Dark Lake on their left and this greatly cheered the mood of Cyr who could not bear to see that stretch of water so distressing for him next to him.

Suddenly, in the distance, at the foot of a steep ridge of a mountain located further north, Anselm saw what appeared to be a small wooden hut, hidden among some large trees that towered over the narrow valley in front of them.

The two walked to that remote home and soon found themselves near it; it was a house made entirely of wood and had a sloping roof with a long chimney pot right in the middle.

Anselm approached the door and, taking a look around, exclaimed:

"Is there anyone?"

No one answered so the knight repeated the question but the result was the same again.

Then Cyr went around the house to see if there was someone inside but it seemed that there was not a soul about.

"Perhaps this is not his home" the dwarf said

"I don't see other houses around here" the knight replied observing the landscape around him

"We should wait here"

"Stay here...I'm going to scour the area around here"

Just as the knight was moving away from there, a voice came from the vegetation on the ridge of that mountain.

Someone was coming down from the mountain humming in a carefree way but, at the sight of the dwarf, he stopped and, drawing the bow, he said aloud:

"Who are you?"

"Hello...my name is Cyr and we are here to talk to Athelor"

"I don't know anyone with that name" the man said pointing the bow at the dwarf

"We don't want to hurt him...we just need information"

"Who are you with?"

"I came here with my friend Anselm" Cyr said pointing his finger at the knight who was out of sight in that moment

"Where is he?" the other asked very suspiciously

"He is looking for *you*...we wanted to know some information"

"I think I can't help you"

"You have a beautiful home, Athelor" a voice said above them

The man turned caught by surprise and, not knowing how to defend himself from the two strangers, he backed away saying:

"I don't know who you are and what you want from me"

"We would like to know something about Kellar" Anselm replied descending the ridge above the hut

Hearing that name, the man had a moment of bewilderment that he was unable to hide but, a few moments later, he recovered saying:

"What do you want to know about that man?"

"We want to prevent him from hurting someone else" Cyr replied

"You won't be able to do it very easily" the man said

"Do you know him?" Anselm asked

"I got to deal with him"

"So...are you Athelor?" the dwarf asked with great curiosity

"Well, yes... it's me"

"King Reginald sends us...he told us that only you can help us"

"I haven't been there for a long time"

"Do you mean Elysande?" the dwarf asked

"Yeah, but...how could I help you?"

"The king told us that you were a prisoner there" the knight exclaimed

"Yes...a long time has passed"

"Well...Reginald informed us that you managed to escape from that fortress through a secret tunnel" Anselm continued

"Uhm...I don't even know if it exists anymore"

"We suggest you joining us to attack Kellar's castle" Cyr said

"And would we be just the three of us?"

"King Reginald's knights will wait for us in the afternoon of tomorrow near the Bluevein's waterfalls"

"Many men will be needed to penetrate the fortress and defeat that killer" Athelor said

"We would be one more with you...and you would make the difference" Anselm replied

"I had to take refuge here to escape that beast"

"We give you the opportunity to stop hiding once and for all" the dwarf replied

"I forgot...how did you get here?"

"We came through the swamps" Cyr said proudly

"It is almost impossible to cross them...no one has ever been able to pass the marshes of Gliness"

"We used a very effective stratagem" Anselm said

"I'm curious to know it"

"We used beech trunks to reach the shore of the Dark Lake" the knight continued

"I think you have been very good"

"By the way...how do you go to the other side?" Cyr asked curiously

"It is very simple...there is a rather narrow passage between the marshes...once I made a map but now I know it by heart" Athelor replied

"Would you be so kind to accompany us down there?" Anselm asked

"I will accompany you to the Intricate Wood"

"Do you mean you will join us?" the dwarf asked

"If the point is killing that cruel man once and for all, I will help you with pleasure"

Cyr and Anselm were very happy for Athelor's decision and that's how the latter invited the other two to his hut, offering them something to eat and drink in large quantities.

After a whole day dedicated to rest and long conversations between the three to tell each other about the adventures they lived, at nightfall the three of them went to sleep with great joy in their hearts.

XVII

When the first timid sunrays appeared across the eastern slopes of the Western Chain, Cyr opened his eyes and saw Anselm and Athelor still sleeping, so he remained on his bed watching from the window the sky changing its colour slowly.

Shortly after, Athelor also woke up and, seeing the dwarf with his eyes open, invited him to go out to enjoy the sunrise in those wild places.

The noise of the two who left the hut also awakened Anselm who thus followed them outside and together they were enchanted for a few minutes by the beauty of the awakening of nature.

After refreshing for a while, the three left that wonderful home and headed for south.

Since they reached the shore of Dark Lake, Athelor showed them the passage through the swamp of Gliness: it consisted of a series of sods of compact and hard soil spaced out a couple of meters from each other and therefore reachable by jumping; the most critical thing was to help Cyr to reach some of these, in fact he found it much more difficult than the other two, but in the end all three found themselves safe on the other side.

Since they went beyond the marshes of Gliness, the three headed for the place where Aster and Cyr's horse had been left and, as soon as they arrived, the horses uttered neighs of recognition towards their riders.

Athelor mounted with Cyr on his horse and so the three galloped to the northeast.

After hours and hours of journey, the three crossed the Plain of the Wind completely and reached their destination in the middle of the afternoon, when the sun was still high in the sky.

Since there was still no one there, the three took advantage to rest in the shade among those rocks that seemed to be excellent hiding places for those who seek a little quiet.

After some time there was a distant noise that made the ground beneath them tremble slightly so Anselm decided to climb one of those rocks and scan the view: towards the south a large dark strip was seen advancing in the plain just towards them.

"I think Reginald is coming with his men!" the knight exclaimed with great euphoria

Cyr and Athelor climbed onto other rocks to enjoy the scene and saw that the huge mass of riders and men on foot proceeded decisively until the same Reginald, who clearly preceded everyone on his horse, was clearly visible.

When they were close enough, the three stood up and began to wave their arms to get noticed.

About a hundred meters away, Reginald detached himself from his army and proceeded towards them galloping at great speed; since he reached the three, the king greeted them and saw that there was a third man with them and immediately understood that Anselm and Cyr had found and convinced that man who could help them.

"I am Reginald, king of Elysande...I guess you are Athelor"

"It's me...it's an honour to meet you personally"

"I am very pleased to see you here to help us, we absolutely needed your help"

"I can't wait to finally get justice"

"Do you remember the precise point where the tunnel access is located?" the king asked

"I remember it as it was yesterday because there, about a couple of meters from that point, there is a large oak tree with huge roots coming out from the ground on which I stumbled, so longing to escape...and I got myself the wound you can see on this arm" Athelor replied

While they were arguing, the rest of the army finally reached their king who introduced Marion to Athelor and took advantage of the moment to reveal the strategy to use; about ten people would have gone inside the tunnel: Anselm, Cyr, Athelor, four bowmen and three men armed with swords.

King Reginald's army was made up of about three hundred men, made up largely of soldiers armed with swords and bowmen, but also about thirty knights and some lancers.

All together they headed for north and, since twilight came, the king's army surrounded the castle, standing a few tens of meters from the walls, under the supervision of Adelard, while Reginald and Marion accompanied the ten who had to enter the tunnel to make sure it was still there and that they found it.

Athelor began to look for the place where the large oak tree was located but the wood was so intricate that it was not easy to find it.

Shortly before total darkness took possession of the forest, Cyr, who wandered here and there without knowing what he was looking for, went to Athelor, who was twenty meters away from him, and led him to the precise point where he had seen that strange oak; it was a very old tree and what made it visible, compared to the other oaks, was precisely the presence of these large roots that came out of the ground as if the tree wanted to free itself and get out of there.

As soon as Athelor saw it, his eyes shone with joy and so Cyr called everyone else saying he had found it.

"Is it this one?" Anselm whispered

"Yes...I'm sure" Athelor replied

The latter then looked at the ground next to the large tree and started making small holes here and there.

Suddenly, while he was digging with enthusiasm, he felt something hard, a few centimeters deep, which resisted the pressure of his hands and, removing the earth that was on it, he discovered entirely what was a real wooden trap door.

The joy in the hearts of all of them was great and Anselm congratulated Athelor who, despite the success obtained, still remained rather cautious since he had no certainty about what awaited them.

Since the trap door was raised, Athelor asked one of the bowmen for the torch and thus saw the wooden staircase that went down a few meters inside that tunnel; he went down and, pointing the torch forward, he could see that nothing had changed since then: it was a tunnel dug into the rocky ground that was about three meters wide and more or less two meters high and was deeply impregnated with humidity.

Athelor beckoned the others to come down, so he was followed respectively by Anselm, Cyr and the other seven men of Reginald.

Entered inside the long tunnel, the ten proceeded with great caution to avoid surprises of any kind.

Reginald and Marion saw the light of the torch grow weak and then disappear completely and so they waited some time there.

After a while they saw a light appear from below and one of the bowmen went up the ladder to warn them that the others had managed to penetrate the fortress, so Reginald and Marion could go to their places and wait for the signal.

XVIII

After covering a long way inside the underground passage, probably a few hundred meters, Anselm, Cyr, Athelor and the others finally found themselves in front of a sturdy staircase that led upwards.

Athelor went up first and, once at the top, raised the heavy trap door slowly, taking a look around to see if there was anyone inside.

Seeing no one, he went up further, thus entering the room, then he invited his friends to do the same and, after closing the trap door, everyone found themselves inside the castle.

It was a practically empty room in which there was only a small window, placed at the top of a wall, that overlooked the internal courtyard of the fortress.

Anselm and the others' bewilderment at seeing that it was an enclosed room without an access, was so great that some of them were already ready to go back, when Athelor indicated to them to wait and not make too much noise.

At a certain point he approached the stone wall on one side of the room and, after waiting a few seconds in silence, he touched a slightly relief stone compared to the others and, suddenly, in front of them all, a part of the wall moved opening as if it were a door.

"How did you manage to...?" Cyr asked

"Shh...let's be quiet! Some guards could be near here" Athelor whispered

Athelor entered the room first and, after seeing that it was empty, he was followed one by one by all the others.

"I've already been here...this is the basement cellar from which I managed to escape" Cyr said whispering to Athelor's ears

"Good for us...I don't remember exactly where this place leads...if you want to go on..." the other answered in an undertone

Before leaving that place, Athelor pushed a stone that protruded slightly on the same wall where that secret passage opened and, with great amazement of everyone, that door closed behind them hiding the secret room.

At the bottom of the cellar there was a staircase that led upwards, so everyone began to climb the stairs following Cyr who, wielding Grin's battle ax, advanced with great caution.

After passing the first storey, Cyr led his friends up the spiral staircase to the floor where he remembered being imprisoned together with Bernard and Faramond and, since he reached the landing, he gestured to the others that that was the door to cross.

The bowmen came forward and, opening the wooden door that separated the stairs from the corridor very slowly, glanced at the latter through that narrow opening.

Two guards were talking to each other at the end of that passage and they did not seem to be particularly attentive when, suddenly, from the bottom of the spiral staircase, there was the sound of footsteps getting closer and closer.

Reginald's men waited for them along the stairs and, as soon as two guards came into their sight, three men of the king, armed with swords, rushed with great speed at the men of Kellar throwing them to the ground and, since they disarmed the guards, they gagged the two sentries leaving them there along the stairs, watched over by two of them.

The attention of the bowmen returned to focus on those two guards along the corridor who, in the meantime, had moved to the spiral stairs and went back and forth continuing to talk to each other.

When the moment was right, the four bowmen came out and, in the twinkling of an eye, threw their arrows at the two guards who fell to the ground without being able to ask for help; immediately all the others came out and scattered here and there except one who remained on guard near the door that led to the stairs.

Anselm and Cyr tried to open the doors of the rooms where their friends were locked up but these were locked; hearing that someone was trying to enter, Faramond understood that something was happening, so he whispered:

"Who's out there?"

"Here we are...Cyr and Anselm!" the dwarf answered hearing his voice

Shortly after Bernard also approached the door and, recognizing the voices of Anselm and Cyr, greeted them from the inside and informed them that only Eustace had the keys; Cyr understood that it was impossible to open those doors with the keys therefore he reported that information to Anselm and the latter decided that those doors had to be forced.

While the two were intent on deciding how to open them, some guards were coming quickly from the lower storey.

As soon as they noticed the situation, they backed away and, taking refuge behind some columns at the beginning of the corridor, they began to shout for help and raise the alarm.

Suddenly chaos broke out inside the castle: a woman came out of one of the corridor's rooms, whom Cyr recognized immediately, and she rushed to Reginald's men who protected her and invited her to stay safe beside them.

Cyr and Anselm greeted Isemay with great happiness and the knight asked her where Evelune was; the woman replied that she had been transferred to another room on the lower floor but did not know exactly where since Kellar kept her in her custody.

Anselm, hearing this news, became very excited and, calling Athelor and two men of Reginald, returned to the inside of the spiral staircase trying to go to the lower storey but some Kellar's guards rushed in and stopped them right on the first floor's landing.

In the meantime, Cyr managed to knock down the door of Faramond's room with his ax and, since the latter was freed, he asked for his help to do the same with that of the room where Bernard was.

The bowmen of the king, meanwhile, held at bay some armed men who tried to access the corridor from the lower floor but they were outnumbered and began to find themselves in difficulty.

Unable to enter the corridor on the first storey, Anselm had to go back upstairs with Athelor and the other two men so that everyone found themselves in the corridor and, when Bernard finally came out of his room, Anselm went to greet his two friends.

Seeing that the situation was going badly, Anselm decided to do the only thing that could save them, therefore he took his bow and, from the window of the room in which Faramond was, he threw an arrow that slit the quiet night air and fell stuck on the ground a few meters from some trees behind which Reginald's soldiers were hidden.

In the twinkling of an eye the king was warned of the signal and therefore he gave the green light to the attack; in a few moments a shower of burning arrows was thrown against the main and secondary entrance of the fortress and, at the same time, an equally large number of darts was launched against the guards who were on the walls, generating chaos and terror between the forces of Kellar.

At that point most of the men headed for outward to defend the walls.

The sky had become a crossroads of arrows that grazed each other and went to all directions causing a continuous hiss that was clearly perceptible in the night.

Some Reginald's men who had prepared some tree trunks, rushed at great speed against the main entrance door, now almost completely burned by flames, to knock it down completely but numerous darts coming from one side of the walls killed all the men of the king, so the entrance remained inaccessible.

Meanwhile, inside the fortress, the bowmen of the king managed to free the upper corridor and, taking advantage of the fact that the guards had rushed out, they headed for the lower floor.

Anselm, Cyr, Bernard, Faramond, Athelor and Isemay had gone down the spiral stairs and, encountering less resistance than before, they entered the lower storey where they began to clash with the numerous Kellar's guards present there.

Some guards of the palace were easily killed due to the fact that they found themselves surrounded by the group led by Anselm on one side, and by the bowmen and armed men of Reginald who had come down the opposite side of the corridor.

Suddenly, Bryce and about twenty men armed with crossbows and swords ran from the lower stairs of the same corridor, forcing the king's men to retreat and remain defensive.

While that hard clash was taking place inside the corridor, from one of the rooms near the lower stairs, Kellar came out with Eustace holding a tied woman on his shoulders, probably fainted, and they were seen running towards the lower floor of the fortress.

At the sight of this scene, Anselm understood that she was Evelune and, if at first his heart rejoiced at the sight of his woman, immediately afterwards he was struck by a sense of anger and tried to encourage his friends to advance to chase the two fugitives.

But the way was blocked by Bryce and his faithful men who proceeded their slow advance inside the passage.

"Hurry up, let's go into the tunnel" Kellar said to Eustace

"Don't you think it will be controlled? In my opinion they discovered the passage and entered from there" Eustace said panting for the run and for the load he had to bear

"It may be that you are right but now it is the only chance of escape that we have!" Kellar answered

Meanwhile, outside, as the bloody clash continued, some of the king's men were sent again to the main door and this time, due to fewer defenders on the walls, they managed to knock down what had left of the door and, at that point, a large number of armed men poured into the walls screaming and creating panic among the enemy forces.

The clash thus became a hand to hand fighting as bowmen and crossbowmen of both sides struck each other in the fray at a distance.

Some bowmen of Reginald entered the castle and began to go up towards the upper storeys, gradually killing the few guards left inside.

Going upstairs, the bowmen ended up in the corridor where a fierce fight was taking place and they found themselves behind Bryce and his men who, taken completely by surprise, were killed one by one.

So, since the corridor was completely cleared, Bernard and Faramond stayed with Isemay and the other men of the king to patrol the rooms and passages of the big palace to make sure that no one had remained hidden inside.

Anselm, who had explicitly requested to be accompanied by Cyr and Athelor, rushed down the stairs to the cellar.

Since the three were inside, they entered the secret room and noticed that the trap door had remained open.

"They passed here" Athelor exclaimed

Anselm and his two friends hurried down the tunnel and they advanced in the pitch darkness until they reached the end of the underground passage.

The trap door had been closed, so, groping in the darkness, Anselm went up the stairs and pulled up the trap door; the three came out of the tunnel to find themselves in the dark again, this time in the middle of the forest.

A man of the king was lying on the ground, probably having been taken by surprise by Kellar while guarding the exit of the passage.

Athelor proposed to split to increase the chance of finding the enemy and Anselm agreed with him.

Advancing in the darkness, Anselm kept an eye on all directions, also peering up into the trees.

Behind him, the racket caused by the clash that still continued outside the castle, contrasted with the dark silence that was in front of him and this made him being in a cold sweat.

Cyr and Athelor had disappeared from sight and the only living thing that he could see in those moments was a big owl that fluttered from one oak to another in an attempt to find a better hiding place.

The knight did not have the slightest idea where he was going but he knew that the two men could not be so far since they had to take Evelune with them.

Suddenly, from a point not well defined, female shouts were heard calling him, Anselm, and immediately afterwards Cyr's voice was heard calling the knight telling him to join him.

Immediately Anselm and Athelor rushed to ask the dwarf where was the more or less precise area from which the voices came.

So the three advanced together and, passing from one tree to another, they felt that their enemy was very near.

Suddenly, about twenty meters from them, two human figures emerged from behind the trunks of some oaks and threw arrows towards the pursuers and then began to run in an attempt to leave behind them.

Then the three began to chase them in an unbridled pursuit until, suddenly, one of the fugitives disappeared from sight and there was a great noise close to him.

When the three arrived there, they saw Eustace and Evelune lying in the middle of a deep hole and so Anselm, deeply moved by the sight of his woman, decided to stop there and drew up his beloved.

"I'll go on chasing Kellar" Athelor said, looking at the knight's eyes

"Okay...can you help me, Cyr?" Anselm asked the dwarf

"Let's draw her up" he replied

While the two were intent on freeing Evelune from that trap, Athelor continued forward in the manhunt.

He heard the other panting and running at a breakneck speed without a precise direction, when, suddenly, the fugitive stopped, perhaps due to fatigue, and, hiding behind a tree, he threw an arrow towards his pursuer.

The dart stuck in a trunk next to Athelor who, with a sudden jerk, hid behind a tree, occasionally protruding his face to scrutinize the enemy's movements.

When Kellar came out of his hiding place to shoot an arrow, Athelor did the same and the two threw their darts almost simultaneously; Athelor was hit in the shoulder and fell to the ground injured, unconscious.

After a few minutes he woke up and, pained, looked at the wound and saw that the arrow had passed from side to side but had not hit anything fatal.

Standing up, he glanced in front of him to see if he could see Kellar but there seemed to be no trace of him; when Athelor took a few steps forward, he saw, behind a tree, Kellar on the ground with a dart that had pierced his abdomen.

Athelor looked at him for a few moments, after which he went back to his friends who were waiting for him near that huge hole.

Cyr took the dart from his shoulder and asked him what had happened to Kellar and Athelor told them that they could find him a few meters away.

So Anselm picked up Evelune, who had not yet awaked, and returned to the castle together with Cyr and Athelor.

XIX

Since they arrived near the walls, the three saw that the assault had ended and the castle had been conquered.

Entering inside the palace, the three saw Reginald and Marion talking with Isemay and, alongside of them there were Adelard, Faramond and Bernard who listened in silence.

As soon as they saw Anselm return with Evelune in his arms, they approached him and, after making sure that she was only passed out, they burst out in a cry of joy and everyone was happy to have survived and to have killed Kellar once and for all.

Shortly after Reginald left the castle with Marion and Isemay to help his injured men while Faramond, Bernard, Cyr and Athelor headed for the courtyard, telling each other what had happened to each of them.

Anselm took Evelune to a room in the palace and laid her on a bed, waiting for her to recover.

After almost half an hour the woman opened her eyes and, at the sight of Anselm in front of her, she allowed herself to be carried away in a cry of joy and finally embraced the knight.

The two looked at each other and a tear fell from Evelune's wet eyes and slid down her face until it fell on the bed.

"You don't know how long I've been waiting for this moment" she said

"It's so great to see you again" he said, fixing her eyes.

The two left the palace and joined the others to help them.

Reginald thanked Anselm, Cyr and Athelor after which he left with Marion, Isemay and his army towards Elysande, bringing with them Eustace, who was locked up in the town's prisons.

Athelor decided to settle in Thedra, so he left north with Bernard, Faramond, Cyr, Anselm and Evelune.

"I will never live hiding again...freedom is too precious to live without it" Athelor said to his friends on the way

"Now you can live as you want" Cyr replied

"I will always be on the side of those who defend freedom, and for this reason I must thank you all"

"We are the ones who have to thank you, Athelor" Anselm intervened

Since then the fortress of Kellar was left to itself and fell into disrepair, becoming a refuge for wild animals.

Since they arrived in Thedra, Anselm and Evelune rested on the lawn outside their home, under the starry July sky.

The two told everything that had happened to them but, after about an hour, they both collapsed into a deep sleep.

In the next morning the two woke up at the first light of dawn and when they saw the Solitary Torrent flow nearby and, further north, the Silver Mount that rose in all its grandeur, they felt at home again and all that they had lived in the previous days seemed now almost distant.

Anselm and Evelune went immediately to the nearby inn of Thedra to visit Athelor and, when the latter left his accommodation, they saw that he was very happy to be there with them and asked him if he needed anything.

"I'll have to look for a house in these days" Athelor said

"We know a man who owns one and would like to sell it" Evelune replied

"I will ask him that"

"I'm going to call Cyr now, so we can all meet here in the inn, what do you think about it?" Anselm proposed

"It seems a great idea! Call Faramond and Bernard too!" Athelor replied

Anselm went to his friend Cyr's house with Evelune and, when they were at the front door, they knocked on it but nobody answered.

Just when the two were about to leave the dwarf's house, they heard the door open and saw Cyr emerge sleepily; at their sight, the dwarf rubbed his eyes and, after making a great yawn, asked them:

"What are you doing here early?"

"It's not so early" Anselm said

"We want to ask you if you want to come to the inn with us" Evelune intervened

"I need to wake up properly" the dwarf replied

"Let's have a cup of milk with Athelor"

"Wait for me a few minutes, I'll join you there"

"Let's go call Bernard and Faramond"

"Okay, see you soon" Cyr said yawning again

Anselm and Evelune found Faramond and Bernard already awake and invited them to join their company and the two gladly accepted, then they found themselves at the inn, until Cyr also joined them, and, as soon as he entered, aroused smiles of hilarity from his friends for the slowness he had when he moved.

While the small group was enjoying that tasty breakfast on that round table laid with food and drinks in large quantities, two stranger figures entered the inn heading towards their table.

At first the group paid no attention to the two, but after they were both a few steps away from them, Cyr glanced at them quickly and, as he was about to look away, he turned once more towards them, exclaiming with great amazement:

"Eluard! Isolde!"

"Here we are" the woman said with great joy

"We are very happy to see you again! What are you doing around here?" Anselm said showing the same amazement of the dwarf

"We are glad too, Anselm! We are here because we have heard of the great victory" Eluard said

"We finally managed to get rid of him...now people will be free to cross the Intricate Wood without any fear" Anselm continued

"Things will change a lot now...we will come more willingly north"

"Sit down...let's have something to eat with us" Evelune intervened

"This is your woman, isn't she, Anselm?" Eluard asked

"I present to you Evelune!"

"We heard about her"

"I already know who told you this news" Anselm said smiling at his friend Cyr

"These are Bernard and Faramond!" the dwarf abruptly cut the subject

After Isolde and Eluard sat down, everyone began to discuss and share the most beautiful events that each of them had experienced, spending the whole day in the crowded inn.

As they delighted in drinking good beer in company, a wind of moderate intensity rose and changed the weather, bringing black clouds laden with humidity from the east.

In the distance, lightning pierced the sky until it dropped on the ground at some point not visible from Thedra and, after a few seconds, it was followed by the disturbing roar of a thunder that attracted the attention of the group inside the inn.

Since everyone realized the sudden change of weather, they decided to leave the inn and each returned to their home; Isolde and Eluard mounted on horseback and galloped at great speed towards the Intricate Wood and subsequently towards their home.

Anselm and Evelune finally entered their home and, exhausted by fatigue, dropped into a deep sleep.

The weather worsened drastically and abruptly and the sky seemed a battlefield, in which invisible powers were warring, launching thunderbolts here and there in a roaring and frenetic chaos.

While human people had abandoned themselves to the oblivion of sleep, in the sky it seemed that the situation was absolutely not the same.

Right in the middle of the night, a shadow approached the house where Anselm and Evelune were sleeping and, stealthily, looked around to make sure no one saw him, and then, with the help of a dagger, he forced the main door and he entered the house.

Advancing in the dark very silently, the figure held the dagger in his hand and headed for the stairs leading to the upper storey.

As the stranger climbed the stairs, strong thunder ripped the sky and rumbled in the valley as if a giant volcano had suddenly exploded; the noise awakened Anselm who, opening his eyes slightly, glimpsed from the window the glow of the lightning that broke right outside.

In the instant between that thunder and another that followed it, a creaking was heard coming from the nearby stairs, so Anselm decided to get up and go to see what it was, sure that it was the current storm that created that noise.

Meanwhile Evelune also woke up, hearing her man walk in the dark, so asked him where he was going and he replied with a nod, intending not to worry.

Suddenly Anselm saw a dark male figure that was a few steps away from him and, screaming, ordered him to stop, frightening Evelune who immediately ran to his side; the human figure, at the cry of the man, immediately fled, heading for downstairs and leaving the house with as quick as lightning speed.

Anselm told the woman to wait for him there and to close the door, then he went out chasing that shadow in the night.

He saw a man jump on horseback with a great leap and so, in order not to miss him, he went to Aster and, in the twinkling of an eye, he began to ride wildly to pursue the fugitive.

When that man realized that he was unable to leave behind his pursuer, he slowed down, turning first his gaze, then his sword towards the other.

Anselm showed himself skilful in his readiness and, unsheathing Aglet, pointed it at that man as a sign of challenge.

The two began to duel in the dark while the storm continued in the sky with great impetuosity; the mysterious knight struck a powerful thrust with his sword which was skillfully warded off by Aglet, but Anselm was forced to move away a few meters to recover and be able to hit his rival.

After a subsequent clash in which the blades of the swords came to beat each other, the two men stopped for a moment to look better and study the opponent.

Before returning to charge, lightning fell from the sky going to illuminate the battlefield of the two duellists showing the face of both of them: the stranger had his head covered by a chainmail that partially concealed his identity, but a detail did not escape the gaze of Anselm who, in fact, remained absolutely amazed: that black horse had an arrow-shaped stain on the muzzle...he had already seen that horse!

Suddenly it occurred to him where he had seen it and, in an incredulous tone of voice, he said to the man:

"So you are..."

"It's me and this time I won't fail"

"I thought Athelor had killed you"

"Your friend had to be a little more careful"

"This time you won't get away with it, Kellar!"

"Look at this sword, because it will soon end your life"

"You knew that at that tournament..."

"Of course...the silver knight was the opponent I had to beat...or kill"

"But the red knight had not been able to do it"

"It will do it now"

Kellar flung himself against Anselm, launching a very violent attack that grazed his rival, forcing him, for a moment, to take a look at the superficial wound that it had caused him.

Returning to the charge, Kellar pointed the blade towards the other and, just as he launched the attack, Anselm struck with his sword the opponent in the abdomen making him fall to the ground with a violent thud.

Seeing that he did not stand up, Anselm dismounted from his horse and since he realized that there was nothing to do for the man, he mounted again on Aster and returned home riding on the prairie now completely wet by the rain that had begun to lash down.

XX

The day after the storm had gone and the sun had returned to shine in the sky, enveloping Thedra in the typical summer heat.

Anselm and Evelune were tiding up the stable where they kept Aster when, suddenly, they heard the sound of hooves approaching them; turning around, the two saw a man on horseback who greeted them and, dismounting from the animal's back, bowed to them and then extended his arm towards them showing a roll of paper:

"This is a message for you, Anselm, knight of Thedra"

"Who are you? And who sends you?" the knight asked

"King Reginald sends me...I am his messenger"

Anselm opened the scroll on which it was written:

"I am very grateful to you, Anselm, son of Alfred, and to all of you for freeing us from the tyrant that infested Intricate Wood and I am pleased to inform you that you will be invited as distinguished guests and participants in the great challenge that we will hold here in Elysande in a week, where the most skilled knight of all will be rewarded by me in person."

king Reginald

"Give my regards to Reginald and tell him that in a week I will be in Elysande with Evelune and all the others"

The messenger thanked the knight and left at a gallop.

Annotations

Printed in Great Britain
by Amazon

24616906R00078